DATE			

THE
MAGICAL
FELLOWSHIP

ALSO BY TOM MCGOWEN

The Magician's Apprentice
The Magician's Company
The Magicians' Challenge
The Shadow of Fomor

The Time of the Forest
The Spirit of the Wild
Odyssey from River Bend
Sir MacHinery

THE AGE OF MAGIC TRILOGY

THE
MAGICAL
FELLOWSHIP

Tom McGowen

LODESTAR BOOKS
Dutton   New York

Copyright © 1991 by Tom McGowen

Library of Congress Cataloging-in-Publication Data

McGowen, Tom.
   The magical fellowship / Tom McGowen. — 1st ed.
     p.   cm. — (Book one of the Age of magic trilogy)
  "Lodestar books."
   Summary: In 30,000 B.C., Lithim, an apprentice magician, and his father set out to unite the warring races of wizards, humans, Little People, and dragons in an effort to save the earth from being destroyed by creatures from beyond the sky.
   ISBN 0-525-67339-3
   [1. Fantasy.] I. Title. II. Series. III. Series: McGowen, Tom. Age of magic trilogy: bk. 1.
PZ7.M47849Maf 1991
[Fic]—dc20   90-45576
                                                  CIP
                                                  AC

Published in the United States by Lodestar Books, an affiliate of Dutton Children's Books, a division of Penguin Books USA Inc.

Published simultaneously in Canada by McClelland & Stewart, Toronto
Editor: Rosemary Brosnan
Designer: Stanley S. Drate
Printed in the U.S.A.   First Edition   10 9 8 7 6 5 4 3 2 1

This one is especially for Alan.

THE
MAGICAL
FELLOWSHIP

Prologue

Five faintly glowing objects were moving through the vast blackness of interstellar space between two stars far out at the edge of the Milky Way galaxy. The objects, moving at a pace considerably faster than the speed of light, were arranged in a precise formation, one behind another, just about seventy miles apart. They were vessels, and each was controlled by a number of intelligent beings within it.

These beings would have been extremely puzzling to human eyes. Their race had achieved highly advanced technology thousands of years before and had begun to control its own evolution, eventually combining muscle and bone with electronic circuitry, so that the present members of the race were now part living creatures and part machines. Their appearance showed this.

The beings were virtually immortal, for although they might be killed by, say, an atomic explosion, they could not die of old age, disease, or ill health. Their intelligence was to a human's as a human's intelligence is to a dog's, so their thoughts, purposes, and goals would have been unfathomable to a human. They were presently embarked upon a sort of titanic engineering project that would literally rearrange a portion of space. Oddly enough, a single small planet of a rather remote star system happened to figure prominently in their plans, and they were proceeding to that planet now to do what had to be done.

The planet was Earth. The time was some two hundred and seventy centuries before the building of the first pyramid of ancient Egypt—a time that would be known to the twentieth century as 30,000 B.C.

Gwolchmig the wizard entered the Grotto of Foreseeing, gathered his bearskin cloak more closely about his bulky shoulders, and ponderously squatted at the edge of the Pool of Vision. The Earth had reached the precise moment that would begin the slow brightening of the sun after winter, bringing another spring and a new year, and the Great Powers—good, evil, and neutral—were momentarily in balance. From this moment until the exact same time the following night, a wizard of high rank would be able to foresee the events of the coming year as they affected him or those whose interests he guarded. As he had done every year at this time for as far back as he could remember, Gwolchmig was about to examine what the future might hold for his people, the Trolls.

He bent forward, huge pale eyes on each side of his enormous snoutlike nose peering into the still, utter blackness of the water. The Pool of Vision was actually a well, a deep shaft that reached down toward the depths of the earth, and it lay at the bottom of the deepest grotto in the vast underground cavern that was the main stronghold of the Northland Trolls. Other wizards used other means, but for Gwolchmig the well was an admirably suitable instrument. He spoke the word of power, which drew together the proper energies. The black surface of the water shivered and began to glow. After a moment, patterns of color started to flicker and flow upon it.

To an untrained eye, these patterns would have been meaningless, but for the Troll wizard, each pattern indicated an event in the course of his world—an earlier-than-usual coming of warm weather this spring, a plentitude of animals for hunting, an exceedingly rainy summer. Motionless and intent, Gwolchmig observed the changing patterns. Once or twice he nodded with satisfaction. Once he made the rasping sound that was a Troll's laughter. Time passed.

Then, abruptly, Gwolchmig stiffened and jerked his massive head closer to the water. He glared in horror at what was being revealed. For several minutes the surface of the water was active with swirls and explosions of brilliance, and then the colors faded to drab grays and browns, which slowly dissolved into darkness. The pool's surface once again became black and still.

Gwolchmig remained poised over the water. He was as badly shaken as it was possible for a member of his race to be. He had just seen a vision of the total destruction of the world within a year's time.

A human's reaction might have been anything from profound grief to hysterical terror. Troll-like, Gwolch-

4

mig's reaction was a terrible rage that such a thing could happen. He could think of his own death, or even the annihilation of his entire tribe, with little emotion, for in either case, life would go on and there would still be a world with Trolls in it. But this promise of the complete and utter obliteration of all Trolls and everything else racked Gwolchmig with bitter fury.

However, the anger quickly gave way to another Troll-like reaction, a fierce resolve to fight back. Future happenings, Gwolchmig knew, were not absolutely fixed; they could be altered, but only with great effort. It was possible that the horrifying event he had foreseen could be changed enough so that the world might not be totally destroyed. But, pondering what might be needed to alter what the Foreseeing had shown, Gwolchmig reluctantly reached the conclusion that not even the all-out efforts of the entire Troll race would be enough.

Licking his thin lips with a pointed purple tongue, Gwolchmig squatted motionless over the dark pool, considering possibilities. There had been certain obscure hints in the Foreseeing that he had ignored at the moment, but now he brought them forth from his memory and carefully examined them. After a time, he realized that they suggested something nearly as startling as the vision of destruction had been and, with growing excitement, he saw there *was* a way whereby the bleak future might be altered. It was a way he would have scoffed at and scorned any other time, but now he was willing to accept it without hesitation. And there was no time to lose in getting started on it!

Gwolchmig stood up. Where to begin? It took only a moment to find an answer to that question, and then he

5

was hurrying out of the grotto, his cape swinging with the speed of his gait.

Few other Trolls were in the cavern's passages at this time of night; most were out hunting and foraging. Those that Gwolchmig passed stared in some surprise at the sight of the aged wizard moving in such haste. He ignored them, hurrying on until he came to a tunnel that wound upward, ending in a small cave that opened onto the outside world. A warrior stood on guard just inside the cave entrance, peering out into the night. Gwolchmig hailed him. "What is the moon's position, guard?"

"Five hands across the sky, Great One," the warrior answered.

The night was more than half over, then, thought Gwolchmig. This meant that what he intended to do would be doubly dangerous, but that couldn't be helped. It had to be done now, tonight, for there was no time to spare.

"I must make a journey," he told the warrior. "It will take perhaps three hands of the moon's course. I want some warriors to accompany me. Four should be enough." He was not overly concerned about his safety while he was heading toward his destination, but speed would be essential and he didn't want to have to stop and deal with any bears, wolf packs, or other creatures that might be tempted to attack a solitary traveler. A party of five Trolls would be sufficient to make virtually anything except a Dragon keep out of their way.

The sentry stared at him with obvious concern. "But—Great One—you will be running the risk of being caught out in the open when the Eye of Day peers over

6

the world's edge!" "Eye of Day" was the Troll term for the hated sun, the light of which meant agonizing death to any Troll caught in it.

"I am aware of that," growled the wizard. "It cannot be helped. Surely you can find some young warriors who are foolhardy enough to take such a risk with me because it will give them a chance to prove their courage!" Proving their courage was, he knew, of prime importance to young male Trolls.

"I will see, Great One," said the sentry in a placating tone. He ducked into a side tunnel that, Gwolchmig knew, led to another small cave used as a guard room. There was a murmur of questioning voices, and shortly the guard reappeared with four warriors crowding behind him. Human eyes would have seen them as squat, gray-skinned, immensely burly creatures with arms and legs as thick as young tree trunks and with huge, pointed ears and enormous noses that took up most of the area of their faces. To Gwolchmig they were fine specimens of sturdy young male Trolls, quite willing, as he had wryly surmised, to risk a cruel death from sunlight for the honor of accompanying him.

"We must hurry," he told them. "Come." Hefting their clubs, they followed him out into the night.

The cave opening was in the midst of a vast evergreen forest, which was covered with the black cloak of night, but to Gwolchmig and his warriors the forest appeared as if lit by a dim twilight, for their eyes, like the eyes of most nocturnal creatures, could gather in even the faintest star-gleams to see by. Moving swiftly in a close single file, the Trolls threaded their way among the trees, from time to time catching glimpses of forest creatures

7

for which, also, the night was a time of activity. However, as the Trolls wound in and out among the shaggy pine trees, they did not even have to use their eyes, for their immense noses, nearly as efficient as the nose of a dog or wolf, were following the scent trail of a well-worn path, which had been used by Trolls for countless centuries. Head down and thoughts on other things, Gwolchmig simply let his nose lead him along, the warriors following silently behind him.

But after some two hours' journey, when Gwolchmig came to a fork in the trail, he turned off the path that was heavy with Troll-scent onto one that had been but little used for a long time. When the warriors realized that he had taken this path, they glanced at one another in some consternation. For this trail ran through a part of the forest that was normally shunned by Trolls. It led to a clearing in which stood the dwelling of a human by the name of Mulng.

Humans and Trolls were ancient and bitter enemies, and under ordinary circumstances any human daring to make a home so near a Troll stronghold would have been turned into vulture meat within a short time. But Mulng was far from ordinary; he happened to be, as Gwolchmig knew, one of the dozen or so most powerful wizards on Earth, and Trolls still growled at the memory of what he had done to the band of Troll warriors that had been sent to put him to death when his presence in the Troll domain became known. Why he wanted to live so near them no Troll could fathom, but they had given his dwelling wide berth ever since he had shown how capably he could defend himself.

"Um . . . Great One?" murmured the warrior directly

behind Gwolchmig, thinking perhaps that the aged wizard hadn't noticed where he was headed.

"I know where I am going," said Gwolchmig gently. He offered no explanation, and the warriors, respectful of his exalted position, did not dare press for one. But he sensed their growing concern as, after nearly an hour more of travel, they neared the clearing. They were also getting worried, as was Gwolchmig, about the sunrise, which was not far off. At the edge of the clearing Gwolchmig stopped and turned to them.

"I will go on alone," he announced. He glanced at the sky. "It is nearing the time when the Eye of Day will appear. We passed a small cave a short way back, where you can spend the day in safety. Tomorrow night, if I have not rejoined you there by the time the moon is one hand high, return to the Hold without me."

One of the warriors held out an entreating hand. "But how will you protect yourself from the Burning Eye, Great One?"

"I hope to spend the day within the walls of the human's dwelling," Gwolchmig replied, to the other Trolls' astonishment. "If I cannot do so—well, it really won't matter. Now go."

An order from their High Wizard was not to be disobeyed. With many worried backward glances, the young Trolls loped off.

Gwolchmig turned back to the clearing. He stood for a time, doing that which was necessary to let the power that clung to him drain away, which would leave him practically defenseless. Then, with the greatest calmness he could muster, he paced unhurriedly into the clearing toward the dwelling, a windowless and apparently doorless, dome-shaped construction of thick logs held together with mortar the color of dried blood.

Some twenty paces away from it Gwolchmig suddenly felt his body begin to tingle sharply and knew that he had set off powerful protective spells that guarded the dwelling and those within it. He halted instantly, knowing that another step might unleash a Bolt of Power against him.

A small, furry shape came pacing around the side of the dwelling and stopped, staring at the Troll with bright, intelligent eyes. It appeared to be nothing more than one of the badgers that inhabited the forest, but Gwolchmig knew it was a Watcher, a creature that had been trained and enchanted by the wizard Mulng. Being a nocturnal animal, it could see in the dark, and Gwolchmig felt sure that Mulng was even now looking through its eyes at him.

Gwolchmig was risking his life in more ways than one. If Mulng should decide that the Troll was attempting some kind of trick and hurled a Bolt of Power against him, the now defenseless Gwolchmig would be destroyed. On the other hand, if Mulng chose to simply ignore him, he would die from exposure to sunlight once the first full flush of dawn lit the sky, which would happen in a very short time. But Gwolchmig was gambling that the human would be so curious about the Troll's odd actions that he would want to investigate and would give Gwolchmig the chance to speak to him.

With the stolid fatalism of his race, Gwolchmig stood waiting for either death or the success of the first step in his plan to save the world.

The boy awoke suddenly, his senses alert. He quickly became aware that every watch and ward spell guarding the house had been triggered.

"Father?" he whispered.

"Yes, Lithim," his father, Mulng, said quietly in the darkness. "Something is inside the clearing. Udgee will be watching it. Look through his eyes."

Lithim concentrated, sending his thoughts through a special pattern as his father had taught him to do when he was only half his present age of twelve. After a few moments, within his mind there was a picture of the area outside the house, seen as if in twilight.

"A Troll!" he exclaimed at the sight of the hulking figure upon which the badger's eyes were fixed.

"Yes," murmured his father. "But that's no ordinary Troll. I'd say it's a full-ranked wizard! There's a trace of considerable power emanating from it, but it appears to have let most of its power drain away for some reason.

It is defenseless against any magical attack, yet it is deliberately exposing itself to one. It's also in danger from the sunrise, which can't be far off. It seems to have deliberately made itself helpless, as if to show that it means no harm."

"But how could it *not* mean harm?" questioned the boy. "The Trolls hate us!"

"Yes," Mulng acknowledged, "but I feel that this one wants to communicate with us for some reason. I'm curious. Let's find out what it wants." Speaking in the Troll language, in a voice that carried through the walls of the house, he called, "Troll mage, what in the name of all the Powers are you up to?"

Gwolchmig answered in the human tongue of the Atlan Domain, of which Mulng was nominally a subject. "Trying to gain your attention, human. Something is going to happen that will be of major importance to both Trolls and humans, Mulng—something that makes our enmity insignificant! I take it you have not yet examined the portents of the future year?"

"No," said Mulng. "I intended to do so first thing in the morning. This is my time of sleep, as you know, and I go about my business in the hours of sunlight, when *you* are abed."

"I urge you to go about that bit of business now," rumbled Gwolchmig. "The portents show that our world is going to be destroyed by the year's end, human, unless we can do something to prevent it. I have come to offer you a truce and my cooperation. I hope you will want to discuss this with me after you satisfy yourself that I speak the truth about this matter." He glanced up at the sky. "But if you wait too long, I fear I will not be capable of any conversation!"

Mulng was silent for a moment. Then he said, "Assist me, Lithim." A small glow of light, about the size of a crab apple, popped into being just over his head, illuminating his lean, bearded face. The boy followed suit with a similar light of his own. Witch Lights, these were called by ordinary folk, because they were the sort of thing much used by village witches to impress people with their power. Actually, such a light was an easy thing to create; Lithim had known how to do it since he was about five.

He followed his father to a rude wooden table made of split logs, which was cluttered with a variety of objects. Mulng took up a clay jar as Lithim slid a shallow stone bowl into position. From the jar Mulng poured a stream of jet-black liquid into the bowl. Then he spoke the word of power and watched intently, as did Lithim, while the black liquid began to glow with moving colors.

When the patterns that had so shocked Gwolchmig appeared, the man's reaction was much like the Troll's had been. His body jerked in surprise and his breath hissed between his lips. The boy was not yet quite capable of fully understanding the patterns of a Foreseeing, but he was able to gain an impression of titanic gouts of fire, immense clouds of steam, and a shivering, shaking, cracking, and crumbling of land. "What does it mean, Father?" he cried.

Mulng did not answer until the liquid went dark. He leaned on the table as if to compose himself. "It means, son," he said in a low voice, "that around the end of the year, some kind of—creatures are going to come from beyond the sky to burn, blast, and reshape the world, wiping out every living thing!"

Lithim considered this in shocked silence. He was, of course, appalled at the thought of the world's destruction, although subconsciously he could hardly bring himself to believe it would happen. But he was even more shaken by what his father had said about the *cause* of the destruction. Lithim firmly believed, as did most other Atlanians, that the sky was a kind of shell, curving over the flat world, and beyond the shell was the vast, endless, cosmic ocean of water, tiny amounts of which were sometimes allowed by the Mother to leak through the shell in the form of rain. But Lithim had never heard his father or any other learned person even speculate on the possibility that anything could or did exist in the cosmic ocean. Such an idea would never have occurred to most people. Yet, apparently, according to the Foreseeing, the creatures bringing doom to the world were coming from *beyond* the sky, *through* the cosmic ocean! It all seemed impossible, but Lithim knew well that a Foreseeing revealed not only that which was possible, but generally inevitable.

"Is there anything we can do?" he murmured, staring toward his father.

In the glow of the Witch Light Mulng's face appeared strained, as if he were wrestling with thoughts. "The Foreseeing shows that these creatures from beyond the sky possess incredible powers," he said. "It seems hopeless. But—that Troll out there apparently has some kind of plan. That's why it came here. It spoke of a truce and cooperation." He straightened up suddenly, as if he had come to a decision. "I am going to let it come in, Lithim. I must hear what it has to say."

"Father!" the boy exclaimed. "It may be a trick!" The thought of letting a Troll enter their home seemed even more appalling than the end of the world!

A brief smile quirked his father's lips. "Think a moment, Lithim. What would be the point for the Troll to be seeking to get in merely to kill us, when it and we will all be dead within a year anyway?" He moved toward a section of wall, which shimmered and suddenly became a thick, thrice-barred door. Mulng lifted the wooden bars, shoved the door open, and stepped out to confront the Troll.

"Come inside," he invited. "I do, indeed, wish to talk with you. You may shelter here until sunset, or longer if you choose."

Gwolchmig lumbered forward, forbearing to emit the sound of relief that wanted to whoosh out of his lips. The sunrise was surely only moments away. This was, he reflected with wry humor, an historic occasion. For probably the first time in history, a Troll had been *invited* into a human dwelling and was going into that dwelling for a purpose other than that of murdering its residents!

Mulng stood aside to let the Troll's huge bulk squeeze past him through the entrance. The man sent a quick thought to the badger, which still stood where it had planted itself defensively before the house—a feeling of warmth and pleasure for the job it had done, a gentle urge for it to now go to its refuge and sleep, a promise of food when it awoke. The badger turned and paced away, and Mulng followed the Troll into the dwelling.

15

He pulled the door shut to seal the interior against sunlight.

Gwolchmig could not refrain from staring about with unabashed curiosity at the dwelling's interior, which was rendered fully visible to him by the Witch Lights of the two humans. Nor could he keep from frankly eyeing them. Gwolchmig had seen plenty of dead humans and had learned the Atlan language from a human captive who had been kept alive for a time for the specific purpose of teaching him, but the Troll still found it interesting to examine the features of a live human up close. He marveled at the incredible smallness, by Troll standards, of a human's nose and eyes and the overall delicacy of the human form. Although Mulng stood a head taller than he, the breadth of Gwolchmig's body was three times that of the human's.

The Troll was also greatly interested in the small human, for he hadn't been aware that Mulng had a companion. He wondered at first if the small human might be a female, perhaps Mulng's mate, but then decided it must be a young, not fully grown human, which was a thing he had never seen. It seemed incredibly fragile, and he suspected that he could easily crumple it up with one of his hands.

Lithim regarded the Troll with equal interest, tinged with more than a little fear. It filled the dwelling like a small mountain; its arms and legs were tree-trunk thick, and the fingers of its three-fingered hands were thicker than his arms. He felt that it could break him into pieces if it wished.

Mulng spoke, using the Atlan tongue inasmuch as the Troll appeared to understand it well. "Obviously you know my identity, as you have called me by name, and unless I am much mistaken, you are Gwolchmig, Wizard of the Northland Trolls, not so?"

"That is correct, Wizard Mulng."

Mulng tugged at his beard, and Lithim sensed that his father was oddly embarrassed by the strangeness of the situation. "This is my son," Mulng said, indicating the boy. "He has the name of Lithim."

Gwolchmig swiveled his head to once again regard the small human. He said nothing to it, for it was beneath the dignity of a Troll of his position to speak to a child, whether Troll-child or human, but now he became aware of the very faint aura of power that emanated from the little creature. "Ah, now I understand why you choose to live so near a Troll domain, where you risk death from those who hate you," he said, turning back to Mulng. "You are training him in wizardry! He has inherited your talent for the art."

"Exactly," Mulng acknowledged, inclining his head. It was necessary in training young wizards that they be constantly under exposure to serious danger in order that their senses be sharpened, and this was precisely why Lithim was being reared in the middle of a forest filled with a number of dangerous animals as well as human-hating Trolls.

Mulng tugged at his beard again. "Er—may I offer you something? Some mead, perhaps?"

The Troll's ears twitched involuntarily, the equivalent, among his people, of a shudder. The thought of drinking the fermented syrup of a sun-drenched plant was repulsive to him. "Thank you, no," he rumbled. "Um— you really need not attempt to observe your kind's usual social customs with me, High Wizard. We are too different from each other for such things to matter. May I suggest that we get right to the purpose of this meeting?"

Mulng nodded. "Indeed." He suddenly smacked a fist angrily against his thigh. "What *are* these things that are coming against us? Gods? Demons? Why do they attack us?"

Gwolchmig was tired from the long walk through the forest, so he squatted on the floor, which was hard-packed dirt, thickly strewn with dried rushes. "Gods or demons they may be," he said. "As to why they attack us, I do not know. All that matters is how they may be prevented from doing what they seek to do. They have tremendous power, and it will take tremendous power to fight them—the power of many wizards and others, working together."

"You spoke of truce and cooperation," said Mulng, eyeing him. "Are you proposing an alliance of Trolls and humans?"

"That, and more than that," replied Gwolchmig, looking steadily back at him. "Trolls, humans, Alfar, the Little People, and even the Dragons, if we can make them understand!" He extended a finger like a stubby tree root and tapped the floor with it for emphasis. "We need *everyone*, Mulng. Everyone who can control magic to the slightest degree; everyone who can use a bow, a spear, an axe, or a club; everyone who can do *whatever* may be needed. Our world is in peril, human, and everyone who lives on it must fight for it side by side or else we shall all perish together!"

Lithim's jaw dropped and he stared in astonishment

at the huge creature. What the Troll was suggesting seemed fantastic. Humans and Trolls had engaged in bitter warfare for centuries. The Alfar, those pale-skinned, silver-haired, vaguely humanlike beings that dwelt hidden in the vast northern forests, had never had anything to do with the other races, looking on them as little better than animals. The Little People, small-statured creatures that seemed a cross between human and wolf, and lived in tribal groups in secluded places, would instantly kill any human or Troll daring to enter their domain. And as for the Dragons, they were gigantic reptiles of strange, alien intelligence that inhabited the higher regions of mountains and were feared by all the other races. All these different kinds of creatures, Lithim felt sure, would no more work together than snow would rise upward back into the sky!

Mulng, too, was staring in surprise at the Troll. Gwolchmig could not read the expressions on the faces of humans, but he sensed their incredulousness. "There was a hint of this in the Foreseeing," he insisted. "A pattern that seemed to show my people and others moving on the same path. I did not understand it at first, but then I realized it was the only way. Think, Mulng—did you not see this, too?"

The human frowned, trying to recall all that the Foreseeing had revealed. An indistinct pattern suddenly reappeared in his mind. "Why, yes!" he exclaimed. "Mighty Mother, you're right! It *was* there—a suggestion that if all the resources of all the races of the world could be brought together, we might just be able to alter this future we were shown!"

19

"Aaah!" The Troll made a groaning sound of satisfaction.

Mulng began to pace. "But you know it will not be easy, Gwolchmig, to bring all the races together, even under these circumstances. There have been too many generations of bloodshed and hatred. Would Troll warriors be willing to fight alongside humans? For that matter, will humans fight alongside Trolls?" He clawed angrily at his beard. "The Alfar *could* be contacted, I suppose. And perhaps even the Little People. But the Dragons . . ." He shook his head. "It hardly seems possible."

"But we ought to try," said Lithim, timidly. He knew he was not worthy of participating in a discussion such as this, between two mighty wizards, but the thought that the world might end, before he even reached his thirteenth summer was horrifying. He felt that he had to do whatever he could to prevent it.

Gwolchmig turned to stare at him, then whirled back to look at Mulng. "Your young one is right, High Wizard," he said. "We must *try*. It is our only hope. I will attempt to make contact with the Alfar, and perhaps you or another human can make contact with the Little People or the Dragons." He extended a massive hand in a pleading gesture. "It can be made to work! Haven't we two come together?"

Mulng regarded him thoughtfully for a moment. He understood fully how the Troll had risked his life to contact a human, and he respected and admired Gwolchmig's determination to fight to save the world. He had also been moved by his son's plea. He reached out his own hand and placed it on the Troll's. This was a gesture of friendship common to both races.

"Indeed, we have come together, friend," he said firmly. "Very well, then. Rest here in safety during the day, High Wizard, and I shall begin making preparations and sending messages. Tonight you can go back to your folk and convince them of what must be done, and tomorrow, Lithim and I will set out on a journey to the isle of the High Chieftain to do the same among our people. I'll have to find someone willing to contact the Little People, and"—he rubbed his chin—"I'll have to start figuring out how I can talk to a Dragon!"

Lithim felt his heart leap, but he did not know whether it was from excitement, hope, or fear.

"Are you feeling any better, Father?" asked Lithim, gazing at his parent with sympathy. Twenty-four days ago they had begun a walking journey from their dwelling in the forest toward the coast, a journey that had been noteworthy for poor food, miserable weather, and aching legs. Then had come a three-day trip in the reeking fishing craft in which they now sat, plowing through a heaving gray sea beneath a dark sky that had steadily poured down rain for the first two days. Lithim had experienced a brief queasiness for a time but had then grown used to the boat's motion. His father, however, had emptied his stomach the very first day, while the boat was still in sight of land, and had been unable to eat, or even think of eating, since. Now he sat beside Lithim, one hand pressed against his belly, the other clutching the edges of his fur cloak together, his mouth pulled down in an expression of discomfort.

"Not really," he replied in a croaking voice. An angry

frown puckered his forehead. "I have truly come to hate those Mother-cursed creatures that are coming out of the sky, not only for what they plan to do to our world, but also for all the unpleasantness they've caused me during this past moon!" He sighed. "Well, at least our journey will soon be over, and I'll be all right once I have my feet on the ground again."

And that won't be long now, thought Lithim, turning to peer in the direction the boat was headed. The coastline of the island of Atlan had been visible since the morning light had been bright enough to see by; now it was late afternoon and the outer buildings of the great port city of Atlan Dis, capital of the empire, could be clearly seen. Lithim had been born there but had been taken away while still a baby, after the death of his mother. He had no recollection of the place and was wildly excited by this visit to it. Mulng, who had lived in the capital for many years, huddled in his furs and rather disinterestedly watched the buildings creep closer.

At last the boat was guided in alongside a lumpy stone wharf, and a sailor hopped across the slim expanse of water between craft and quay to wrap a rope of twisted leather around a stone stanchion. Mulng gripped his bag of possessions in one hand and his wizard's staff in the other and rose unsteadily to his feet. Lithim sprang up, seized the bag and wooden chest that he was responsible for carrying, and waited for his father. Mulng nodded to the fishing boat's captain, received an answering wave of the man's hand, and stepped off the boat onto the landing, followed by the boy.

The wizard stood for a few moments, taking slow,

deep breaths to try to get the last of the queasiness out of his stomach and to grow accustomed to the motionless ground beneath his feet. Lithim peered in all directions, trying to see everything at once. Then, "Come along, son," said Mulng, and together they trudged into Atlan Dis, capital of the Atlan Domain.

There were scores of villages scattered throughout the mainland portion of the Domain and several dozen on Atlan Isle itself—mostly collections of rough huts made of logs or dried, woven grass plastered with clay, populated by a few score to a few hundred persons. But Atlan Dis, at the edge of the Western Sea, was a giant metropolis of some two thousand people, with many impressive buildings constructed of massive stone blocks. Most impressive of all was the High Chieftain's hall, a hulking square structure that rose to a height some four times that of a tall man. It stood in almost the exact center of the city, with the other buildings clustered helter-skelter about it, forming a maze that baffled any stranger trying to find his way to anywhere. But Mulng knew the city well, having served his seven-year apprenticeship in it and then having practiced as a wizard for a number of years before taking his baby son away into the great forest of the northern mainland. He easily threaded his way among the houses, taverns, and other buildings, heading steadily toward a particular dwelling, which was his destination.

Lithim, of course, was a typical rustic visitor from the outlands, staring at the buildings and thronging people with awe-filled eyes. Having grown up with only his father for company, he was particularly intrigued by the women he saw, many of whom had their lips painted a brilliant red with an expensive cosmetic that came, via merchant traders, from the vast continent that lay beyond the Southern Sea. He noted with interest the savory smells coming from eating places he and his father passed and eyed with admiration a pair of sauntering Chieftain's Guardsmen wearing leather tunics covered with overlapping disks of auroch's horn and carrying spears tipped with smooth, sharp, leaf-shaped stone points that were masterpieces of the flintchipper's art. Grinning with delight, the boy took in all these sights, sounds, and smells of civilization—then sobered suddenly, as he recalled that, according to the portents of the future, all this life and liveliness could be obliterated within a year's time!

At length, Lithim and his father came to an impressive dwelling with a door that bore characters burned into it that stood for the name "Gling," and here Mulng came to a stop. With the butt of his staff he gave the door three resounding knocks, followed by a short pause and then a fourth knock, which served notice that a fellow magician had come to call. Leaning on his staff with his bag over his shoulder, he waited until the door was slid open by a rather scrawny young apprentice with an enormous beard. "High Wizard Mulng and son to see Wizard Gling," Mulng told him. The young man bowed and stood aside for them to enter.

They then followed him down a short, dark corridor and into a large, square room illuminated by a crackling fire in an open fireplace and a number of smoky oil lamps set in niches in each wall. To Lithim, the room seemed dominated by the tall, heavy man who stood with hands on hips in front of the fire. He had a round, red face and a shock of pure white, gossamer-fine hair that seemed to be trying to float away from his head. With the firelight behind it, it looked like a halo. Because of the warmth of the room, the man was wearing only a leather kilt.

"Mulng!" he boomed, grinning. "Good to see you again!"

"It is good to see you, too, Gling," Lithim's father replied with a smile. He indicated the boy standing beside him. "This is my son, Lithim."

Lithim bowed respectfully and the big man regarded him with a thoughtful expression. "You take after your mother, boy," he remarked. "The last time I saw you, you were a babe in arms and your father was taking you off to the Troll borderland to rear you as a wizard." He glanced back at Mulng. "How is he progressing? I sense considerable talent."

"He does have considerable talent," Mulng answered, a tone of pride in his voice.

"Fine, fine." Gling put his hands behind his back and began to rock back and forth slightly on his feet. "Well, sit you down and let's talk about these Mother-cursed Sky Things that are coming to slaughter us. When I did my Foreseeing and observed what the coming year had in store for us, I was tempted to just forget about everything and use the year to do all the eating and drinking I could before they got here. Then your messenger bird arrived and your message gave me hope. Have you actually made an alliance with *Trolls?*"

"With their High Wizard Gwolchmig, at least," said Mulng, who seated himself on a bench near one wall and was joined on it by Lithim. "A very interesting person. I found him quite likable."

Gling gave a grunt that indicated doubt. "Perhaps. I'm inclined to go along with the old belief that the only good Troll is one that's lying stiff on his back with a spear in his gut. But I suppose it will be useful to have Troll mages working with us on this problem. The Mother knows, we'll need all the help we can get!"

"Were you able to contact all the other mages here, as I requested?" Mulng asked.

"Oh, yes. I've presented your plan to every high-level mage in the city—Ulnr, Kteng, Natl, and the rest. They all feel it offers the only hope, just as I do."

"What of the High Chieftain? Will he give us the help we'll need?"

Gling hesitated. "The High Chieftain's attitude is . . . peculiar," he said after a moment. "Kteng and Natl and I went to see him right after your message arrived, to advise him of what the Foreseeing had shown us all and to tell him of your suggestion for trying to avert the doom. He was horrified and concerned and seemed ready to do everything you were urging. But then, a few days later, when I went to talk with him about some specific things, such as contacting the people across the Southern Sea or the eastern Horse People to join our efforts, he acted very differently. He was . . . cold, aloof, made me feel like a sneaky apprentice who's been caught trying to steal his master's best spells! He refused to discuss any of the things I wanted to talk about and simply ordered me to instruct all the mages here on Atlan to assemble before him on the last night of Spring-moon to discuss the matter then. Inasmuch as that's today, I'm mighty glad *you* showed up this afternoon."

"So am I," said Mulng, frowning. "I don't like the sound of this, Gling. What could be bubbling in his mind to make him behave that way?"

"Who can fathom the mind of a chieftain?" said Gling, quoting an old proverb. "I suspect, Mulng, that politics have somehow intruded into the situation."

"Politics? What have politics got to do with the end of the world?" Mulng exploded. "Mighty Mother, we're facing the greatest crisis that ever was! Not even the worst war, the worst drought or famine, and the worst pestilence all striking us at the same time could be the equal of *this!* A Troll saw clearly what has to be done; can't a High Chieftain see it? A High Chieftain's *job* is to lead his people in time of trouble; that's what he's mainly *for;* doesn't he understand that?"

"This one's not much like his father, whom you knew so well, Mulng," Gling said. "He's really not very bright."

To Lithim, this talk of the High Chieftain of the Atlan Domain was both exciting and faintly shocking. He had always pictured the ruler of all Atlan as a remote, imposing figure, dwelling in a golden room and surrounded by guards and servants. To learn that his father had known such a personage "well," as Gling had stated, was an exhilarating surprise. But to hear his father and Gling speak disparagingly of the High Chieftain was a less pleasant surprise, for it seemed to indicate that the mighty ruler was apparently just an ordinary man and presumably not a very smart one!

Mulng sighed, pressing the palm of one hand against

his stomach. "Gling, could you give us something to eat? I threw up everything in my stomach from seasickness three days ago, and I've had no food since, and I suspect Lithim is hungry, too."

"Of course," murmured the Atlanian, and stepped out of the room. Shortly he returned, bearing two bowls of mead and followed by the young apprentice, who carried a platter piled with smoked fish, which he placed on the bench between the man and boy. Lithim found that he had a better appetite now that he was back on land, and his father, of course, was nearly starving, so they began to wolf down the food eagerly.

"What are your thoughts on these Sky Creatures?" queried Gling, watching them eat. "I went through all the old writings I possess, as well as all those I could borrow from other mages, but I could find no references at all to anything like them. They aren't even mentioned in any of the religious writings in the Books of the Mother." He shook his head. "Things from beyond the sky. It's incredible!"

Lithim looked at his father. During their long journey, Mulng had often discussed the puzzling Sky Creatures with the boy, and Lithim knew the conclusion Mulng had reached about them. It was a fundamental teaching of the religion of Atlan that the world itself was a goddess, the Mother, who had created both herself and all the living things that dwelt upon her, and that she was the only world there was. Like most people of the Atlan Domain, Mulng had generally accepted that teaching, mainly because there was no real evidence to contradict it. But the coming of the Sky Creatures had led him to an inescapable change of mind. "I think they come from another world, Gling," he said, looking up at the other man. "That's the only possible answer. The Foreseeing indicated they were traveling in some sort of boat or craft, but they couldn't have just been floating about in the Deep forever; they must have come from somewhere. There must be other worlds beside ours floating in the Deep, and these things have come from one of them."

What his father had just uttered was heresy, and Lithim watched Gling with some apprehension to see how the man would react to it. But Gling merely nodded. "That's pretty much the thought I've been flirting with, but I guess I was reluctant to come right out and admit it." He cocked his head. "Mulng, I'm sure it has occurred to you, as it has to me and others, that this Foreseeing casts a great deal of doubt on many of the teachings of the priestesses of the Mother. That doesn't bother me much; like a lot of people, I don't take everything the priestesses say at face value. But what effect will this have on the kind of people who *do* believe everything that's written in the Book of the Mother, I wonder?"

"I've wondered about that, too," said Mulng. "It will upset them, I should think. And it may cause trouble of one sort or another."

Gling nodded again. His face took on a look of rapt interest, and he fondled his chin thoughtfully. "What would another world be like, do you suppose?" he wondered, obviously fascinated by the idea. "Probably very different from ours, eh? These creatures certainly seem to be very different from us. I got the impression from the Foreseeing that they were partly made of *rock!*"

"Yes, I got that impression, too, and so did the Troll mage, Gwolchmig," said Mulng. He took a drink of mead and wiped his mouth with the back of his hand. "A kind of smooth, shiny rock, somehow merged with flesh! They seem to be unlike any living thing we know of."

The bearded apprentice came into the room, carrying a tunic, cloak, and footwear. "The sun is nearly down, Master," he announced, holding out the garments to Gling. "It will be darkfall soon."

Gling took the clothing from him and, plumping down onto a bench, began to draw one of the furry, calf-length boots onto his leg. "Let's be off to the hall of the High Chieftain and find out what's on his mind. He wanted us all there by darkfall."

Mulng rose to his feet and stretched. "I'd love to find a steamhouse and have a long bath first, but . . ." He shrugged. "As you say, it's fortunate that I arrived in time to be able to attend this meeting so I can see for myself what's troubling the High Chieftain." He looked toward Lithim, still seated on the bench. "Lith, I think perhaps you should come with us."

Lithim had expected to be left behind in Gling's house, for he was only an apprentice and this was to be a meeting of the top wizards of the realm. But now, after all, he would get to see these great people, see the inside of the High Chieftain's hall, and see the High Chieftain himself. Beaming with delight, he leaped up from the bench.

4

A few minutes later they were striding along through the shadows that were gathering in the narrow pathways between the city's stone buildings, heading toward the looming structure in the distance, the hall of the High Chieftain. Not surprisingly, they shortly encountered a trio of mages heading the same way. Two of these were men, Ulnr and Kteng, whom Mulng had known when they were all young apprentices, and the third was a youngish woman named Natl, who seemed quite pretty to Lithim, with tawny blonde hair and green eyes. These mages greeted Mulng with exclamations of delight that he had arrived in time to attend the meeting called by the High Chieftain.

Reaching the great hall, they found that the door had been slid aside and light was streaming through the entrance, painting the street with a broad patch of pale orange. Entering, the five mages and the boy came into a vast rectangular room, ablaze with the light of numerous torches in rows of stone holders along each wall and crowded with scores of magicians of all degrees—residents of the city as well as many from various communities on the island, and even one or two who, like Mulng and Lithim, were visitors from the mainland. Warriors of the High Chieftain's guard stood at their posts along the walls, looking bored. Running the entire length of one wall was a three-step-high stone platform, upon which stood an elaborate chair, the back and sides of which were formed of huge, curved tusks of *mammoots,* the giant, furry, long-nosed beasts that roamed in herds in the far northern wastelands. Seated in this chair was a man who, Lithim knew at once, must be none other than Tlon, son of Mleng Bearslayer, High Chieftain of the Atlan Domain. He was tall and burly, with curling auburn hair and beard and piercing blue eyes, which were roving over the room. His face was impassive, but the longer Lithim studied him, the more the boy felt that the High Chieftain was masking an inner hostility, directed toward the people filling the hall.

Gathered at the foot of the platform, beneath the throne, were half a dozen women in ceremonial robes made of plaited dried plant stems dyed red and black. They ranged in age from middle years to elderly. Lithim had seen such a woman once when he had accompanied his father on a trip to the human community nearest their forest home, and Mulng had pointed her out as a Daughter of the Mother, a priestess of the state religion of the Atlan Domain. As Lithim gazed curiously at this bevy of priestesses, he realized that they, too, were registering hositility toward the crowd of mages but, unlike the High Chieftain, they were making no attempt to conceal it. Puzzled, the boy turned toward his father to see if he, too, had noticed the attitude of the man and the group of women.

Mulng had. "I think I can guess what caused the High Chieftain's change of mind," he said softly to Gling, who was standing close beside him. "There's something going on between him and the Council of Priestesses. Look at them."

"I fear you're right," the Atlanian wizard agreed after a moment. "Mulng, this may be some of that religious trouble you said you were afraid of."

"Mighty Mother, with the most horrifying calamity that has ever happened staring us in the face, are we now going to have to stop to argue about statements in the Book of the Mother?" growled Mulng.

On the platform, Tlon shifted his feet, cleared his throat, and drummed his fingertips on the white curve of a *mammoot* tusk that formed an armrest. He was clearly impatient, and after a short time passed during which no other mages entered the hall, he signaled to a guardsman to push the door shut and rose to his feet. The rumble of conversation in the hall quickly broke off. Tlon swept the crowd with his eyes and spoke.

"I have called you all together to speak of this matter of 'demons from the sky' that you claim to have foreseen coming to destroy our world. This is a curious and incredible prophesy. Are you all indeed agreed upon it?"

There were murmurs of assent, in surprised tones, from the crowd. Many mages were staring in consternation at the High Chieftain. His use of the word *claim* had shocked them, for he seemed almost to be implying

34

that the mages of the Domain were *lying* about what they had foreseen.

At the obvious unity of agreement of the assembled magicians, Tlon's lips grew noticeably thin. "You all insist that this was, without a doubt, the meaning of what was foreseen?" he barked.

The men and women exchanged puzzled and uncertain glances, but no one answered the High Chieftain's question. "Well, someone's got to throw a spear and see what it sticks in," muttered Mulng. "High Chieftain," he called, raising his voice so that it carried through the hall, "that which was foreseen has been agreed to by every mage in the Atlan Domain as well as some outside. This has been made known to you; yet it is clear you have doubts. May we know why?"

"Who are you?" Tlon demanded, glaring at him. The High Chieftain's voice was like a knife jab, sharp and savage.

"I am the High Wizard Mulng, from the eastern border of your domain."

"Mulng. Oh, yes." Lithim felt that the High Chieftain was looking at his father as if he would like to stab him with his eyes. "My father often spoke of you. You did him several services, I believe."

"I was proud to serve your father. I hope to serve you as best I can in this terrible crisis that threatens us."

The High Chieftain's lips thinned again. "Is it to serve *me* that you demand that all the resources of the Atlan Domain be put at the disposal of you and your fellow mages? Did you feel you were serving *me* when you took it upon yourself to make a treaty with our greatest enemies, the Trolls?"

Lithim's heart began to pound. There was no doubt but that this man who ruled all of the Atlan Domain was angry with his father! The boy sensed danger.

Mulng kept his face expressionless. "High Chieftain, I most certainly did not intend to make any 'demands.' It was but an ardent request, prompted by the need to move *fast* to avert this terrible thing that threatens us. We are facing the end of the world unless we can—"

"Enough!" Tlon snapped out the word. "I have heard all that from your emissary, Gling, and others. You ask why I have doubts. I will let a representative of the Mighty Mother answer you." He looked down at the cluster of priestesses. "Daughter Chuln."

One of the priestesses stepped forth. She was a small, plump, gray-haired woman of about his father's age, judged Lithim. He heard Gling whisper hastily to his father: "She runs the priestesses' council. They do what she says. Beware of her; she's as deadly as a poisonous snake!"

The woman paced forward until she was face-to-face with Mulng, no more than an arm's length between them. Eyeing her from beside his father, Lithim noted that her round face and small, sharp features made her look remarkably like an owl.

"Wizard Mulng," she said suddenly, in a surprisingly pleasant voice, "what is the Mother?"

Why is she asking Father *that?* wondered Lithim. It was the sort of question one might ask a very young child. There was a standard, traditional answer to it, and Mulng gave this. "The Mother is the earth."

The priestess nodded. "Correct. The Mother is the earth. The kindly earth, who clothes herself in green

36

food so that her children may eat, and who brings sweet waters eternally coursing down the mountainsides, so that her children may drink. The all-powerful earth, who brings forth flowing fire from the mountaintops, who calls forth raging storms from her cloak, the sky, and who makes the very rocks shake and split, to remind us of her power!" Her voice had risen dramatically, and now she let it drop, almost whispering her words to Mulng in a manner that dripped with contempt. "Do you truly think she would let herself be rent and made barren as you say you have foreseen? Do you really think she would let her children, whom she has cherished and nourished since the beginning, be wiped away, as you say you have foreseen?" Her voice shot up again, nearly to a scream. "Dare you think that *She*, the Maker of All, could be *destroyed,* as you say you have foreseen?"

Mulng's face was impassive. "I gave no thought to any religious significance of what I saw, Holy Daughter. I saw what I saw—the destruction of the world and its life. That is what the Foreseeing showed"—he lifted a hand and gestured at the crowd of mages about them—"to me and to all these others."

"You were mistaken," she said coldly. "All of you."

This was comparable to telling an experienced hunter that he had no skill, or a master flintchipper that his work was clumsy. Lithim saw fury kindling on the faces of the men and women mages as the priestess's insult sank in.

"The magical talent that permits you to make such a statement is not apparent to me," sneered Mulng. He was insulting her back, making the point that inasmuch as she wasn't a mage, she didn't know what she was talking about.

But she shrugged off his derision with unconcern. "Oh, it is true that I am no mage. But there are mages among the Daughters, and competent mages, as you well know. They, too, watched the Foreseeing, as you did. But they did not, of course, interpret it in the same blasphemous way!"

"I am not aware that there can be more than one interpretation of the truth," said Mulng. "But pray, tell me and all these others what their interpretation was."

"It was this." The woman's eyes grew bleak and her mouth hard. "We *do* face a terrible threat—a horrifying threat! That is true. But it is not from any so-called demons from beyond the sky; that is nonsense. It is from enemies that are *outside the Atlan Domain and the Mother's embrace*—the murderous, Motherless Trolls, that have slain and tortured the Mother's children since time unremembered, and the proud, sneering, Mother-hating Alfar, and the foul Dragons! The Foreseeing showed that they will band together in an evil alliance to destroy humanity! There will be blood and fire and death and destruction throughout the Atlan realm, but in the end, the Mother shall give victory to her children, and the forces of evil will be wiped off her body!"

Mulng was staring at her, consternation showing on his face, and Lithim wondered what his father was thinking. What Mulng was thinking was that it was incredible that anyone could have made such a stew of nonsense out of the things the Foreseeing had shown, but he realized now that for anyone who held such rigid, narrow beliefs as the Daughters of the Mother, a true evaluation of the Foreseeing was impossible. They could not admit the reality of the creatures from the sky, for in their belief, the Mother had created only creatures of earth. They could not admit that the world might be destroyed, for that would mean that their very goddess herself could be destroyed. And so, they had simply twisted the whole meaning of the Foreseeing to fit their beliefs and were accusing the mages of Atlan of having misinterpreted it!

Almost as if she were reading his mind, Chuln pressed an attack on this very point. "It is not surprising, I am sorry to say, that most of the mages of the Atlan Domain made only a superficial evaluation of the Foreseeing and ignored its true meaning." She turned from Mulng and glowered at the crowd around them. "Mages are not noted for their knowledge of the Mother and devotion to her ways! But now that you know the truth, I command you to recant this foolishness of 'Sky Creatures,' and this blasphemous talk of the world's destruction, and"—she turned back to glare at Mulng—"these questionable dealings with enemies of the Mother and of Atlan! Give your skills and powers to the High Chieftain for the campaigns he will soon launch to catch our foes unaware. Dedicate yourselves to the service of the Mother, for with her help, Atlan will prevail!"

Her speech finished, she continued to fix Mulng with a stony gaze. He inclined his head slightly but said nothing. Chuln dropped her eyes to look bleakly for a moment at Lithim. He felt that he wanted to shudder, but forced himself not to and met her eyes steadily. After a moment, she turned away.

39

The voice of the High Chieftain broke into the stunned silence. He had reseated himself in the great chair, both arms flat on the *mammoot*-tusk armrests, his legs widespread—a pose that radiated power and self-assurance.

"Now you have the answer, High Wizard Mulng, and all you others, as to why I changed my mind," he said. "Once Daughter Chuln and her mages explained the real meaning of the Foreseeing to me, I put aside all my fear of Sky Creatures and world's end and turned my thoughts to the real problem, that of defending the Domain against the onslaught of the Trolls and others who will seek to destroy it. And all of you—all of you—will be called upon to aid in that defense." He gave a condescending flip of his hand. "Mulng, out of remembrance of your services to my father, I shall ignore your role in this affair. I am sure that you did what you did out of concern for the Domain—although I am rather surprised that you let the Trolls so easily trick you into that pledge of a treaty. However, it is forgotten."

He stood up. "Now hear me all. I declare this matter of Sky Creatures and the 'end of the world' is closed. Far too many people have heard of it and have been disturbed and worried by it, so let there be no more talk of it! I have spoken. That is all."

He turned and, trailed by his guards, marched along the platform to a flight of stone stairs that led to his living quarters, over the main floor of the hall. A warrior slid open the door of the hall and silently, in a close cluster, the Daughters of the Mother passed through it, their plaited robes swishing. As she exited, Chuln cast a hard-eyed glance at the assembled mages of the Atlan Domain, standing in stunned silence.

5

Lithim was appalled! He had never dreamed that a tiny handful of people, such as the priestesses, could have the power to block something that was a matter of life and death for the whole world! When he and his father had set out on their journey to Atlan, the boy had been filled with the elation of hope. He had complete faith and trust in his father's wisdom and magical skill, and he was sure that Mulng, with the help of Atlan wizards, would be able to do what was needed to forge the great brotherhood of human, Troll, Alfar, Little People, and Dragons, who could weave their combined magic into a weapon to fight the Sky Creatures and save the world. Now, in a matter of seconds, Lithim's hope had been snatched away by this group of powerful people, the priestesses and the High Chieftain, who refused to accept the truth because it threatened their power and authority. Lithim was enraged to the point of tears by the unfairness of the situation.

Obviously, some of the mages were also angered and appalled. Gling gave vent to a loud snort of contempt. "So we're just to ignore the end of the world because the Daughters assure us it can't happen, eh? Friends, have you ever before encountered such stupidity?"

"Now, just a moment," a mage standing near him said sharply. The man was a stocky, dark-haired magician of lesser degree from a remote village on the island. "We all know that any Foreseeing is subject to more than one interpretation. With all due respect to High Wizard Mulng, I fear many of us may have been stampeded into a wrong interpretation by his prodding, sincere though he may be. The Daughters' interpretation certainly makes more sense to me, now that I have been made aware of it. After all, how could the *Mother* be destroyed?"

Natl, the yellow-haired woman mage, turned angry eyes on the man. "If the Foreseeing showed that the earth can be destroyed, then it *can* be, and that is what the Foreseeing showed, deny it though you will! Saying that a thing is light when it is really dark does not change the fact that it *is* dark. The world *will* be destroyed unless we do something to avert the destruction!"

"I will not listen further to such heresy!" shouted the dark-haired man. "I regret I was drawn into it in the first place." He turned and stalked off.

"I wonder how many others feel as he does?" drawled Gling, as if mildly curious.

"I do, for one," Kteng announced, belligerently eyeing the tall man. He turned to Mulng. "Mulng, I'm sorry, but I, too, have changed my mind about this matter. It is my counsel to all of you to obey the decision of the

High Chieftain and the Daughters, for your own good and for the good of the realm." He stared pointedly at Mulng. "What do you intend to do?"

"Me?" Lithim's father smiled affably. "Well, my son and I have three days' chill of a sea voyage clinging to us, and ever since making landfall this afternoon I've been wishing I could take a good, long steam bath. So that's what I intend to do. Gling, Natl, Ulnr, will you join Lithim and me?"

Lithim understood that his father had extended this invitation to the three mages who hadn't changed sides, while deliberately excluding Kteng, because he wanted to talk about how to deal with the stumbling block that had been hurled down by the High Chieftain and the Daughters. A steamhouse would be a perfect place for holding an absolutely private conversation—and hatching a plot.

"There's a steamhouse not far from here whose owner owes me for some things," said Gling. "The four of you come with me there, as my guests." They left, ignoring Kteng, who stared suspiciously after them, painfully aware that his company wasn't wanted.

The steamhouse was right at the edge of one of the canals that wound through the city, so that patrons could use the canal as a swimming pool after their baths. The owner welcomed Gling and his party and escorted them to a large bath-dome that could accommodate five or six persons. They undressed outside, squeezed in through the tiny entrance, and squatted in a circle around a small, deep pool of water that filled a pit in the center of the dome's floor. An attendant, a boy of about Lithim's age, squirmed through the entrance, gingerly pushing a clay bowl full of large stones that had been heated red-hot in a fire. He upended the bowl, dumping the stones into the pool, where they hissed like a dozen angry snakes and sent up clouds of steam. The heating and bringing of stones had always been Lithim's task when he and Mulng had taken baths in the tiny bath-dome near their house in the forest, and Lithim now luxuriated in having someone else do this task for *him*. The attendant withdrew, sealing the entrance. The air at once began to grow hot and thick with steam, and Lithim leaned back in the darkness to let the heat seep into his body. He would not enter the conversation the four mages were going to have, of course, but he was content to know that he would be part of whatever plan they worked out. He had the exciting feeling of belonging to something great and important!

"All right," said Gling, speaking first. "It's obvious that we, at least, have no doubts about what the Foreseeing really showed. Now, the question is, do we keep on trying to do whatever we can, despite the High Chieftain and the cursed Daughters, or must we give up?"

"Of course we can't give up," Lithim, with satisfaction, heard his father say. "We might just as well cut our wrists open and bleed to death! As long as there is the slightest chance that we can do something to keep the Sky Creatures from carrying out their destruction, we must try!"

"I think most of the mages who were there tonight would say the same," commented Natl. "From what I know of them, there are only a few like Kteng and that other fellow who take the Mother-worship seriously enough to go along with Chuln and her gang of vixens."

"I agree," said Gling. "Very well, then, do we just keep on with things as planned and tell Tlon and the Daughters to go chew worms?"

"I don't think we dare be openly disobedient," Ulnr objected. "Tlon would put every single mage in the Atlan Domain under death edict if he felt they were defying him, without caring what the consequences might be. And he'd have the backing of every Daughter in every temple in the Domain, who would probably be able to turn many of the people against us, as well. We'd simply get a lot of ourselves killed or imprisoned and wouldn't be able to accomplish a thing toward averting the catastrophe."

"Well, there's always the possibility of taking the High Chieftain out of the picture," Gling suggested, a trifle hesitantly. "The four of us could probably work up a spell to make him waste away—"

"I wouldn't want to do that," said Mulng quickly. "No, I think our best course is to make a *show* of obedience, to pretend that we're going to obey the command of the High Chieftain and the Daughters— and to keep right on doing what we intended to do, in secret! We must get in touch with all the mages we know for sure are still in agreement with us about what the Foreseeing showed and get them working secretly on ways of fighting the Sky Things. We must find those willing to act as emissaries to the mages of the kingdoms and tribes across the Southern Sea so we can work with them and exchange ideas. We should try to get in touch with the Horse People in the east. We must manage to stay in contact with the Trolls, and if Gwolchmig is successful in gaining the help of the Alfar, as he was going to try to do, we'll have to open communication with them—all this secretly, of course." He sighed. "Curse Tlon and the Daughters for making everything so difficult, but that's how it will have to be."

"Are you going to stay in Atlan Dis and help get all this set up?" questioned Natl.

"I'm afraid I can't. You three will have to get it started. I promised Gwolchmig I'd try to get in touch with the Dragons, and that means a long and difficult journey that I'd better start soon."

Gling gave a questioning grunt. "Contact with the Dragons? Is that really possible? They won't even have contact with one another, except at mating time. Would any of them be willing to converse with a human?"

"We have to find out," said Mulng. "We have to try. Their magic is of a different kind from ours, and they could be immensely helpful. As Gwolchmig said, it's their world, too, and they're facing annihilation with the rest of us, so that may make them willing to listen to our plan. But we really won't know what they'll do unless someone tries to talk with one of them, and I've decided that must be my main task." He hesitated a moment, then said, "Gling, can Lithim stay with you while I'm off trying to do it?"

Lithim had been half dozing in the steamy warmth, but as his father's words penetrated his consciousness, he came fully awake, his body jerking forward. "Father! I thought I was going with you!"

"No, Lith." Mulng's voice came softly through the darkness. "It's much too dangerous a task, and as long as there's the slightest possibility that we might defeat these Sky Things, and you'll have a chance to live, I don't want to expose you to any more danger than necessary. You can become a really great wizard, and Gling can help you very much."

"I'll be honored," said Gling, his loud voice not covering up his emotion at having Mulng entrust him with the care of his son.

Lithim had come to like the rough and hearty Gling and wouldn't have minded staying with him, but the boy was dismayed and hurt by his father's decision. He had never been apart from Mulng in all his twelve years of life, and he felt they certainly shouldn't be apart now, when there might be less than a year of life left to them. He cast about desperately for an argument that would make his father change his mind.

"What's the difference if there's going to be danger searching for the Dragon mage?" he asked. "I've been in danger all my life in the northland forest. You always said it would help me become a better wizard!"

"It's not the same," Mulng told him. "That was the *edge* of danger; this will be danger's very heart! I've got to cross through land where the Little People roam; then I've got to make my way up a mountainside, through some reportedly deadly spells laid down by a Dragon wizard whose magic may well be superior to my own. If I make it to the top and the Dragon is even there, I don't know whether he'll listen to me, step on me, or have me for a meal. But if I were to get killed and you were with me, you'd be left alone and helpless, and your chances of surviving would be very slight. I can't risk that. I must know that, whatever happens to me, you'll still have a chance to survive if the world can be saved."

"But you'll need help," Lithim protested tearfully. "I could help you!"

"I know you could help me," Mulng said, and Lithim could hear the pride in his voice. "And I wish with all my heart I could take you with me. But I don't dare. Please don't ask to come with me anymore, Lith; it's hard enough for me as it is."

Lithim unwillingly subsided, and there was an uncomfortable silence in the steamhouse for a few moments. Then Natl said, "But your son is right, Mulng—you will need help. This is a gigantic task, even for a wizard as capable as you. You could use the help of other mages."

"Yes, I could," he agreed. "And I had hoped I could find two or three who'd be willing to risk their bodies to go along with me. But that was before Tlon and the priestesses threw water on the fire. Now the only mages I feel I can really trust are you and Gling and Ulnr, and you're all needed here to set up our secret operation."

"Gling and Ulnr can easily do that without me," Natl said. "I'd be willing to go with you, Mulng. I know I'm only a low-ranked sorceress, but I could be of some help."

"I'm sure you could," said Mulng after a moment. "But as I explained to Lithim, Natl, this is going to be a Mother-cursed dangerous thing I'm trying to do."

"I understand that," she said earnestly. "I can accept it. It could be my chance to do something really important, Mulng! All I've done with my magic up to now is things like preparing love potions for homely girls, and casting locator spells to help stupid merchants' wives

48

find lost necklaces, and putting stay-fresh spells on the water jars of fishing boats. I'm able to do a good many more useful things than those, but there's no call for anything more here for me. If I could use my talents to help you contact that Dragon mage, I'd feel I had really *done* something!"

"Well—all right, then," Mulng agreed. Unseen in the darkness, Lithim scowled. It was bad enough that he was being left behind, but it was even worse to think that this stranger-woman would be sharing the dangers with his father that he should be sharing! He distrusted her. Perhaps she was really just trying to make his father become fond of her!

The heat inside the steamhouse had reached its maximum, and perspiration was pouring off everyone's body. "I've had enough steam," Gling gasped. "I'm ready for my swim. Let's make the rest of our plans over a bowl of mead and a platter of meat at some good eating place!"

Ulnr, squatting nearest the entrance, unsealed it. One at a time they wriggled out of the dome, sprinted the short distance to the canal, and flung themselves into the delightfully cool water. They swam and sported for a time; then Gling bellowed, "How about that mead and meat?" and struck out for the bank. The others followed. They padded to the huge, roaring fire in which the stones were being heated, and attendants gave them clumps of dried moss with which to pat themselves dry. In time, they collected their clothing and mage staffs, dressed themselves, and made their way out into the winding streets of the city.

The city lay shrouded in inky darkness, but at many

of the points where streets crossed, huge torches flared—logs of resinous pine wrapped with cobwebs and thick with gluey sap, they would burn for most of the night, providing beacons and welcome patches of light in the darkness. Gling stopped at the foot of a stone pillar that held one of these torches, and the others gathered about him, black and orange forms in the flickering light.

"There's a place up that way that's called One-Eyed Tlun's," said Gling, pointing. "The food is pretty good, and—"

Lithim whirled, facing out into the darkness. His entire body was tingling, from the activation of a protective spell that his father had placed on him years before. Yet somehow Lithim knew that the main danger was directed at his father. He flung himself in front of Mulng, who was just turning, crossed his wrists over his chest, and shrieked "Avert!" There was a puff of flame and a shower of sparks in the air before him. Someone had flung a spear out of the darkness, and Lithim's shouted spell, plus the spell protecting him, had just barely incinerated it before it could rip into his father's body!

Natl struck her staff against the ground and activated a Spell of Light. For several seconds the area in a circle some fifty paces around them was illuminated as if by a bolt of lightning, and just at the edge of this field of brilliance they all saw a figure, several spears clutched in one hand, scuttling off down one of the narrow pathways between two rows of houses. Then darkness snapped back, replacing the light.

"He was trying to kill you, Father!" raged Lithim.

Mulng put his arm around the boy's shoulders. "Yes, son. But you saved my life."

"Let's get out of this torchlight," urged Gling, herding the others into the darkness. "He might come back for another try."

Several paces away from the torch they huddled together, barely distinct shapes to one another and completely invisible to anyone who might be lurking in the distant darkness. "I don't think he'll come back," muttered Ulnr. "He'll be afraid we might put an unpleasant spell on him!"

"Who would want to kill you, Father?" Lithim demanded.

"Yes, do you have any enemies here that you know of?" questioned Gling.

"I haven't been in this city for twelve years," said Mulng, "and I don't think there was ever anyone here who disliked me so much they'd want to kill me after that long a time. For that matter, they probably wouldn't even know I was here. And I certainly haven't been back in Atlan Dis long enough, or done anything, to have made any enemies except"—he paused a moment and sighed—"except Tlon and Chuln. I suppose either of them could be behind this."

"That's what I think," Ulnr agreed. "I'd say Tlon was responsible. That spearman was skilled, and if he wasn't one of Tlon's guardsmen, then I'm a Troll!"

"Chuln could have gotten a guardsman to do it, too, if she could convince him the Mother favored it or some such thing," rumbled Gling. "But there's little doubt it was either her or Tlon, and that means you have a serious problem, Mulng. One of them wants you dead so that you can't cause trouble over this matter of the Foreseeing, and inasmuch as they didn't get you this time, they'll try again. I think you'd better leave Atlan immediately!"

"Yes," said Mulng, and Lithim's heart sank. He had thought he would still have his father for a few more days before Mulng had to leave on his journey to locate a Dragon mage, but now it sounded as if Mulng would be leaving at once. This was confirmed by what he said next. "Natl, if you still want to go with me, how soon could you be ready to leave?"

"Why, all I really have to do is throw some things into a bag or two and put a seal-spell on the door of my house," she answered. "I could be standing on the dock, ready to leave, by sunup."

"Then we'll meet you on the dock at sunup," said Mulng. "We'll make a deal with the first crew we can find that's sailing for the mainland to take us on as passengers."

Lithim's heart began to pound. His father had said, "*We'll* meet you on the dock—"

Mulng's hand closed gently on the boy's shoulder. "Lithim, this changes everything. I don't dare leave you here now because Tlon or Chuln could use you as a hostage against me, or they might even kill you out of spite! It seems you'll actually be safer with me than you would be here." He squeezed the shoulder. "Besides, you handled yourself very well just now, when you kept that spear out of my chest! I don't think I have to worry about you as much as I thought I might. I believe you and Natl and I will make a good team of Dragon seekers!"

6

His heart singing, Lithim accompanied his father to the docks the next morning with the gray light of dawn just creeping into the streets of Atlan Dis. Natl was waiting for them, squatting beside a bag and chest, which contained her possessions. The dock area was already bustling with the activity of the crews of fishing boats and other vessels making ready to sail on the morning tide. The three travelers made inquiries and were fortunate enough to find a merchant ship sailing for the northern coast of the mainland with a cargo of salt gleaned from the sea that lapped Atlan's shores— one of the island's main industries. By the time the sun was a red ball several finger widths above the horizon, the ship was under way and Atlan Dis was receding from sight.

It wasn't long before Mulng's seasickness struck again, and he retreated into the tiny area below the deck that had been set aside for the three travelers. Natl turned out to be as good a sailor as Lithim, and so the boy found himself sharing her company most of the time. He was shy at first, for he was not at all used to women, and he was also still distrustful of Natl for having volunteered to accompany his father. But Natl seemed enormously interested in hearing accounts of his life in the northland forest, and before long he found himself recounting some of his major adventures there, such as the time he had encountered an angry bear, which he had frightened off by creating an illusion of a wall of fire in front of himself, and the time he had lain hidden among some bushes and watched a mortal combat between two young male griffins. Natl listened wide-eyed.

"I envy you, Lithim," she told him. "I grew up in a quiet little village on Atlan Isle, where nothing *ever* happened, and I went to Atlan Dis when I was twenty summers old and have lived there ever since. You've seen a lot more than I have, even though I'm almost three times older than you!" Lithim discovered that he was beginning to like her.

On the fourth day of the voyage, Mulng joined them to watch the northern coastline of the mainland draw closer. His face was pale and his expression sour. "The Mother's curse on Tlon and Chuln and their assassins for making me suffer all this again so soon," he growled.

"We'll be ashore before long," Lithim tried to console him. "You'll be able to rest awhile until you feel better."

Mulng shook his head. "No time to rest. We've got a long way to go and we must get started at once."

In the port city where they went ashore, they joined a salt caravan that was headed inland toward the east. At the caravan's first stop, a village some seven days distant from the coast, they separated from the salt merchants, turning northeast. Ten days later they trudged through the south gate of the village of Soonchen, their destination. Thus, from the day Lithim and his father had started out, the world was a month and a half closer to what mages were calling "the Earthdoom"—the time when the alien creatures would arrive.

Soonchen village stood at the edge of a small lake at what was roughly the northeastern tip of the Atlan Domain. It was a collection of some sixty log-walled, bark-roofed buildings of varying sizes, surrounded by a high wall of logs and a moat filled with water from the lake. From the square towers that formed the corners of its walls one could see what appeared to be a strip of purple-gray haze spread across the horizon; this was actually a range of mountains known as the Graystones, in which a number of Dragons were known to dwell. The mountains were about eight days distant from the village, but three days before reaching them, one would enter a hilly region in which bands of the Little People hunted. It was the nearness of these tiny, barbaric creatures that made Soonchen's wall and moat necessary.

The three travelers made their way to the village's single guesthouse, a building that provided sleeping accommodations for travelers who had nowhere else to stay, and were assigned a small room. Leaving their bags and chests well protected by spells, they then searched out the village's sole mage, a dark-haired, pleasant-faced woman by the name of Hlim. Drawing her out with a few questions, Mulng determined that she was a firm believer in the reality of the Earthdoom which she, too, had foreseen, and was living in despair at the

55

thought of the coming end of the world. Once he was sure she couldn't be swayed from her view by any arguments of the Daughters, who of course maintained a temple in Soonchen, or by any order from a chieftain, Mulng told her of the secret efforts being made to alter the future.

"Mighty Mother be thanked that something is being done," she said tearfully. "Is there any way I can help?"

"That's why we've come to you," Mulng told her. "Natl and Lithim and I intend to go to the mountains. I have to try to make contact with a Dragon known as Klo-gra-hwurg-ka-urgu-nga, but my sources of information about him were so old I'm not even sure he's still alive. Anything you could tell us about him, or about the Little People, would be most helpful."

Hlim stared at the three of them with obvious concern. "Three humans—and one but a child—trying to make their way through the lands where the Little People hunt? This is a fearful thing you plan to do, High Wizard Mulng! It is necessary, at times, for the people of this village to get building stones, pine logs, and other things from the mountains, and this is always done by parties of at least forty armed men—and they usually lose three or four going through the place of the Little People!"

Mulng said: "Well, actually, we're hoping there will be a few more than just the three of us, Mage Hlim. I asked the people who manage the guesthouse to put out word that we want to hire a few experienced warriors. I feel that perhaps five or six good warriors backed by two competent mages—and Lithim, too, has some useful skills—might even get through more easily than a larger group could."

She nodded, although somewhat doubtfully. "Well, let me see what I can find out about your Dragon."

She went to a long shelf that held a number of birch-bark scrolls. She sorted through these until she found the one she wanted. It was brittle with age, and she unrolled it carefully.

"Yes, here it is," she said after a moment. "As of sixty summers ago, that Dragon you have named was known to be dwelling on the mountain that's called the Old Woman. He was apparently fairly active then, so chances are he's still alive; the creatures live for many hundreds of years. According to this source, which happens to be my own grandmother, his lair is ringed with spells for both attracting food animals and repelling enemies. He seems to be a mage of considerable power."

Mulng nodded. "That's why I must try to talk with him. Very well, what you tell me matches my own information, and inasmuch as there's a good chance he's still alive, it's worth making the effort to reach him. Now, what can you tell us of the Little People that may be of use to us?"

"They live in family groups of from fifteen to twenty or so," she said. "Each group has a dwelling that's a wide, round pit about four man-lengths deep. The pits are roofed over with many straight, trimmed branches to form a cone; the branches are covered with woven, dried grass mats, and those are covered with earth and growing grass, so that from a distance the roof of a Little People dwelling looks like a small, pointed swelling of the ground. Watch for those, and stay well away from them."

"How do they get in and out of such dwellings?" Lithim asked, curious and eager to learn as much as he could about these creatures.

"There's a hole in the point of the cone, with a ladder reaching up to it," Hlim told him. "It lets in air and lets out the smoke of cooking fires. The family group hunts by day, all together. Each group has its own territory and it never crosses into the territory of another group. Everything is food for them; they'd be just as happy to eat *you* as they would a bird or a rabbit! However, they do not hunt or eat wolves, which are sacred to them. They believe they are descended from a wolf, which they worship."

"Interesting," Mulng remarked, "and perhaps very useful to know. How do they hunt?"

"They creep up close and throw spears. The spearpoints are smeared with a poison that acts very quickly. They also set snares for small animals and birds and dig pitfalls for big ones." She hesitated a moment. "It is believed that they also make use of magic. Spells to bring animals close to where hunters are hiding, spells to make a herd of animals panic and run across a place where a pitfall has been dug—that sort of thing. We really don't know exactly what they may be capable of, but it is suspected that there may be some very powerful mages among them."

"Then they, too, might be of great help in our efforts to fight the Sky Creatures," said Mulng. He pursed his lips thoughtfully. "Perhaps, as long as I have this opportunity, I ought to—" Seeing the expressions on the faces of Lithim and Natl, he broke off, smiling. "I know; first things first, and first we must find our Dragon." He rose from the log stool on which he had been seated while Hlim talked. "Our thanks to you, Mage Hlim. You have been very helpful."

She gave him a wistful smile. "I wish I were braver, so that I could offer to go with you. May the Mother smile on you in this dangerous task you are undertaking."

Leaving Hlim's dwelling, the man, woman, and boy made their way back along the dusty lane that led to the guesthouse. Lithim's mind was working, his thoughts moving along a path that had been suggested by something Hlim had said. "Father—what Hlim said about the Little People holding wolves sacred—couldn't we use a shape-changing spell to make us look like wolves to them so they wouldn't attack us?"

Mulng clapped him on the shoulder. "Exactly what I was thinking, Lith! That may be a way of getting through their lands without any trouble."

Nearing the guesthouse, they saw that a group of men was squatting near its entrance. Unmistakably warriors, each man bore a flint-tipped spear and an oval shield of wood covered with thick leather. Mulng hailed them. "I am the High Wizard Mulng. Are you perhaps seeking me?"

The men scrambled to their feet and moved forward to gather around Mulng, Lithim, and Natl. The eldest of them, a dark-haired fellow of some forty summers, offered a grin with a number of gaps in it and spoke. "Yes, indeed, High Wizard. We heard as that you were a-wanting some skilled hunter-warriors for a little journey you wished to make." He swung a hand in a broad arc that took in the other four men. "Here's the band of Rlna—my band. It's the best you'll find in Soonchen!"

Lithim eyed the warriors with interest. He had seen others like them the few times he had gone with Mulng to visit the village nearest their forest home, and his father had explained how such men made their living. They were mercenaries, who could be hired either to do the hunting for their employer or to fight his enemies. Most of their work consisted of supplying meat to butchers and hides to tanners, but if a local chieftain had to make an attack on a troublesome band of outlaws, or mount a defense against the raids of Trolls, or even settle a dispute with a neighboring village, men such as these formed the bulk of his army. When there were no contracts for meat or skins, or no battles, these men fed themselves with their own hunting, or perhaps even hired themselves out for tasks requiring pure muscle, such as the cutting down of trees and the hauling of them to a carpenter's workplace. It seemed to Lithim as if this would be an interesting and exciting way to live!

Mulng, too, was looking the men over, and he liked what he saw. They appeared healthy, which meant they were good hunters, and their weapons were well cared for, which indicated they were experienced fighting men.

"I have no doubt at all that you're as good as your leader says," he told them heartily. "But let me lay things out where you can plainly see them. I must tell you that it's to the mountains we want to go, which means we must get through the territory of the Little

People. We will be well covered with protective spells, but even so, we may have to fight off a hunting party or two. Anyone who chooses to come with us will be rewarded for the risk."

The warrior-leader's grin had faded when he heard the words *Little People,* but after a moment it returned. "Well," he said, "fighting is what warriors are for, and we've all been into Little People territory a bit, and without any spells to help." He cocked his head, looking interested. "What sorts of spells, High Wizard?"

"By day, from a distance beyond about fifty paces from us, we'll appear as a small pack of wolves trotting along," Mulng informed him. "The Little People don't hunt wolves or bother them, I'm told, so that should keep hunting parties from paying any attention to us. By night, when we're sleeping, we'll seem to be piles of rocks, low shrubs, or patches of herbs. Someone would have to get close enough to fall over one of us to find out what we really are. And if we should get into a battle, there are a lot of things that I, and Sorceress Natl, and my son, Apprentice Wizard Lithim here, can do to make things difficult for our opponents. We can make them see three or four of each of us, so they won't know who to throw spears at, or we can put a ring of fire around us that they can't get through—many things."

The mercenary leader glanced at his companions. "Those sound like useful tricks, eh, boys?" He looked back at Mulng. "Perhaps we might all be willing to risk it, High Wizard. But what about that reward you mentioned?"

Mulng grinned. He pulled a leather pouch from his

belt and poured a number of gleaming, irregular objects into his palm—gold nuggets that had been hammered into rough disks. These, and more, had been given to him years before by High Chieftain Mleng, Tlon's father, in payment for services Mulng had done him. Mulng had had no need for money in the northland forest and had even let Lithim use the disks for playthings when he was a toddler, but they represented considerable wealth. "One of these for each man now, and one for each when we return. In addition, I will give each of you a spell that can call any kind of animal you seek into the range of a spear throw. And, of course, we'll provide all the food for the journey."

The gold was as much wealth as these warriors could otherwise hope to gain over a period of several years, while the spell Mulng had offered would guarantee each man's success as a hunter for the rest of his life. Rlna gazed into the faces of his men and read eager agreement on each. "Done, High Wizard," he said. He spat on his palm and extended his hand. "By the Mother's approval."

Mulng spat on his own palm. "By the Mother's approval," he said and clasped the other's hand so that their spittle mingled. An unbreakable bargain had been sealed.

"Good," said Mulng. "Take your first payment, go have some fun, and we'll meet at sunup tomorrow by the north gate, ready to set out."

Lithim felt a thrill course through his body at his father's words. Tomorrow, he knew, would be the real beginning of the greatest and most dangerous adventure that he might ever have.

7

"I have noticed during my lifetime," remarked Mulng, with a distinct tone of bitterness in his voice, "that a long journey always begins on a gloomy day."

Lithim suspected that his father's belief wasn't necessarily true, for he distinctly remembered that the long journey he and Mulng had made from their forest home to Atlan Isle had begun on a very bright and pleasant day. For that matter, he thought, if you counted their departure from Atlan as the actual beginning of *this* journey to find a Dragon mage, it had also been a sunny day. However, whether today was actually the middle of a journey or the beginning of one, as his father chose to regard it, Lithim silently agreed that it *was* gloomy. The sky was a solid gray mist that hid the dawning sun and poured down a steady, chill drizzle. Lithim, Mulng, and Natl, seated beside the still-closed north gate of Soonchen among the numerous bags of provisions they had purchased the previous day, wore cowls of sealskin that protected their heads and shoulders and huddled in their fur cloaks.

When the warriors began to arrive in ones and twos, several of them were also cowled, but others were bare-headed and actually seemed to appreciate the feeling of the cold rain splashing on their skulls—probably because, Lithim suspected, they had thundering headaches from drinking all the mead they could buy with the gold his father had given them. Rlna, wearing a cowl and seeming a bit less bleary-eyed than the others, helped his men strap on the sacks of dried meat, ground acorn meal, and other provisions. Mulng, Lithim, and Natl had already helped each other put on shoulder bundles that contained personal belongings and items they needed for the journey. Their bundles were no less bulky, although Lithim's was a bit lighter than those of the warriors. The warriors were also, of course, burdened with their weapons and shields.

By the time each man had his pack satisfactorily arranged so that it could be shrugged off quickly if need be, the village guardsmen had unbarred and heaved open the huge doors of the gate, after first having scrutinized the surrounding countryside for any sign of enemies or dangerous beasts. Seeing that all the warriors were ready, Mulng trudged through the gate, Lithim and Natl at his side, and the warriors fell in after them, several exchanging crude pleasantries with the guardsmen, who watched them go with curiosity.

A short distance away from the village wall, Rlna ordered his men into a battle-ready formation. "Tlal, take the forward point; Tkuln and Ulnda, take the flanks; Gdeng, take the rear."

Young Tlal objected. "Why get into formation now, Rlna? We're a good four days from the Little People's territory."

"Well, there just might be a Little People hunting band out here somewhere that doesn't *care* how many days away it's supposed to be," growled his leader. "So get your nose up to the front and keep your *eyes* open!"

The men took up their positions with no further objections. Rlna stayed beside Mulng, Natl, and Lithim, apparently having detailed himself to act as their guard. After a few moments, he began a conversation.

"It's none of my affair, wizards, and you can tell me to tie a knot in my tongue if you don't wish to talk about it, but I am most curious as to why you want to be a-going to the mountains. There's nothing there I know of except for rocks and trees and a few Dragons you'd likely not care to meet."

"Well, that's not exactly correct," Mulng answered him. "As a matter of fact, I'm going there especially *to* meet a Dragon." Noting the sudden look of apprehension on the man's face, he quickly reassured him. "You and your men won't be involved. You can just make camp and wait while I try to find the one I want to talk to."

Rlna shook his head in obvious admiration. "I bow to you, wizards. You've got a lot more liver than many a warrior I've known to try a thing like that! But may I ask why, in the Mother's name, would you *want* to try to talk with a Dragon?"

Lithim could see that his father was considering how to answer this question and hoped he would give the warrior-leader a full explanation. Of course, High Chieftain Tlon had ordered all mages not to speak of the Earthdoom to anyone, but let *him* go chew worms, thought Lithim darkly. The boy was convinced it had been Tlon who had sent that spearman to try to kill his father!

To his satisfaction, Mulng explained everything. "Rlna, I'm sure you know that at the end of every year most mages perform what is called a Foreseeing and look into the future to see what the coming year holds," he said. "Well, at the last Foreseeing, every mage in the Atlan Domain, as well as Troll mages and probably all others, too, saw something dreadful. Some kind of strange creatures are going to be coming out of the sky at the end of the year, and they will try to destroy our world. But most of us mages think that if we can all work together—humans, Trolls, Alfar, Little People, and Dragons—we may be able to prevent this from happening. So I'm going to see if this Dragon, which is a powerful mage, will help us and will ask other Dragon mages to help us."

Rlna stared at the wizard in silence for a few moments, his mind obviously churning over what he had just been told. Despite the incredibility of an attack by unknown creatures from the sky, he did not doubt the truth of Mulng's words, for a mage would not lie about such things. "Mighty Mother, this is a heavy thing you've given my mind to hold, High Wizard," he said at last. "Heavier by far than the pack on my back. The end of the world in less than a year! But—you mages think you can prevent it, eh?"

"We'll do our best," Mulng assured him. "That's why I'm trying to get to that Dragon."

The warrior nodded. "We'll do *our* best to see that you get there," he murmured. Shortly, he sidled off to begin talking animatedly with one of the men out on the flank.

"They'll all know about the Earthdoom by midday," observed Lithim.

"It's only fair that they should," stated Mulng. "They're playing a rather important part in this whole thing, too, and they ought to be aware of it. It will make them feel like more than just hired men."

The rain stopped a little before midday, and the sky lightened a bit but stayed a uniform misty gray. The spring grass was still short and sparse, and their feet made squishing noises on the wet ground. In the distance they saw a herd of horses running, their hoofs sending up silvery showers as they passed over puddles.

"It would be nice if we could ride on horses like the Horse People of the east do," remarked Lithim, "instead of having to walk everywhere."

"It would also be nice if we could have a couple of haunches of horse to roast for our midday meal," suggested Mulng, eyeing the distant creatures, "but they're too far off for a spear cast and moving too fast for a summoning spell to work. We'll just have to be content with porridge."

He called to Rlna to stop for a meal. They were moving alongside a narrow, shallow river that ran down from the mountains to empty into the lake at Soonchen, so water was plentiful. They all carried wooden bowls among their personal belongings, and their luncheon consisted of bowls of acorn meal mixed with water to form a tasteless but nourishing porridge—typical travelers' fare. The warriors were full of questions about the Earthdoom which Mulng and Natl answered honestly and completely, without the least concern that they were committing treason and heresy by ignoring the commands of the High Chieftain and the Daughters of the Mother.

The sky cleared even more in the afternoon, and eventually the sun came out. Fortunately, there was no rainbow visible; that would have been an omen of bad luck. They saw another herd of horses, or perhaps the same one, and a herd of long-horned, hump-necked bison. A large flock of cranes flapped by overhead, heading north.

They tramped on until sunset. Mulng and Natl took a reading of the surroundings as best they could with only the limited magical equipment they had brought. They determined there was no danger and decided a campfire could be lit to help them dry off. Their supper was dried, salted meat, washed down with water from the river.

While eating, they heard the howling of a wolf pack far in the distance. Before they settled down to sleep, Mulng walked in a wide circle around them all, chanting and touching his staff to the earth in a precise pattern. When he was finished, any animal that might attempt to cross the invisible circle he had made would activate a spell that would cause it to see and feel a wall of raging fire around the humans. No sentry was necessary, to the great satisfaction of the warriors.

They were astir before sunup and on the move when

the sky was bright enough to show the way clearly. It was another gray day, and by afternoon it was raining again. The rain kept on until well into the night. The third day also dawned gray but did not yield any rain. The fourth day was bright and clear, and in the distance they could see the hills that lay in the territory of the Little People.

They reached the border of Little People territory shortly before midmorning of the fifth day. It was clearly marked; a long, heavy log lay across the trail that ran along the river, and perched upon the log were seven human skulls in a row. The tops of the skulls had gaping holes in them.

"A border marker provided by the Little People themselves," explained Rlna. "You can't say they don't give fair warning, eh, wizards?"

"Why are the skulls all broken open that way?" inquired Lithim, staring in horrified fascination.

"The brains of humans are a delicacy to the Little People," said the young warrior named Tlal. "They break open your skull and scoop out the brains to eat, you see."

"Before or after they kill you?" asked Natl with a straight face, causing Lithim to giggle.

"Well, the sooner we're in, the sooner we'll be out," commented Mulng. "Let me set up the spell that will make the Little People see us as wolves and we can get started. Natl, while I'm doing that, will you take a reading to make sure no one is observing us from afar?"

The two mages went about their tasks, watched in silence by the five warriors. Lithim assisted his father.

Finishing, Mulng looked questioningly at the sorceress. "Anything?"

She shook her head. "Nothing but rabbits, gophers, and a few snakes, for apparently thousands of paces in all directions."

"Fine. Let's go, then. I'll take the lead; Lith, I want you right behind me. From now on, don't anyone talk unless you must, and then only in a whisper."

He stepped carefully across the skull-decorated log, followed by Lithim, then Natl and the warriors. They grouped loosely together and began to move at a rapid walk that was almost a trot. To themselves, they looked the same, but Lithim, his father, and Natl knew that anyone or anything viewing them from more than fifty paces away saw a good-sized pack of eight lean, gray wolves, trotting purposefully on their way.

They kept alongside the river, which wound among the hills. The land of the Little People, it appeared to Lithim, was in no way different from any other land; in fact, it was a most pleasant place, the boy thought. The hills were green with the fresh vegetation of spring and the clusters of trees were pink and white with blossoms. The mountains looming in the distance had now become resolved into hard-edged shapes, their sides mottled with the dark green of pine forests and the purple gray of bare stone, their tips glinting white with snow. Lithim thought he could make out the mountain of their destination, the one called the Old Woman because the odd configuration of its peak seemed to form the profile of a crone with hooked nose and turned-up chin.

They stopped briefly at midday, but merely to gulp water from the river, for they dared not take the time for a meal, and if they clustered together to do so, they might draw attention to themselves. But throughout the entire day they saw nothing but a small herd of animals, so far in the distance it was not even possible to tell what kind of creature they were. Sunset came, and with it a slight sense of safety, for the Little People were not known to prowl at night. Still, the travelers could not risk building a fire, of course, and they silently gulped down their supper of dried meat in darkness. Mulng softly muttered the spell that would make them blend into the landscape while they slept and also surrounded them with the circle of false fire that would be activated by any creature venturing too close to them.

Well, thought Lithim, lying curled on the ground between his father and Natl, we've survived one day in the country of the Little People. All we've got to do is survive three more!

8

At the first light of morning they took a quick "breakfast" of water and started out at once. It was another bright and beautiful day, and Lithim was momentarily surprised to hear his father grumbling about it.

"Fog!" growled Mulng. "Three straight days of fog—that's what I'd rather see than all this sunshine. Fog, that I could gather and build with, to hide us in safety!"

It seemed as if Mulng had foreseen trouble, for it was midmorning when luck suddenly deserted them. Lithim became aware that his body was tingling with the warning of danger, indicating that the protective spell covering him had been activated by something. He stopped in his tracks. "Father!" he whispered sharply.

Mulng, too, had been alerted. He glanced about and realized that they were all veering away from the river. "Hold!" he ordered.

They all stopped except for the warrior named Gdeng, who was farthest out on the flank and did not,

72

apparently, hear Mulng's whispered command. He trotted on, not quite conscious of where he was going. Something was tugging at him, urging him to come to it, and it was pleasant to simply follow that urge with no thought.

"Hunting magic," Mulng whispered savagely between his teeth, watching Gdeng's figure recede. "He is being pulled toward someone, and I couldn't stop him in time." He swept his eyes across the four warriors. "There is nothing we can do. He's a dead man, and we are dead, too, unless we get out of here fast!"

Grim-faced, Rlna nodded. He fought against the urging that sought to pull him after Gdeng and began a lurching run in the opposite direction. Herded by Mulng and Natl, the warriors staggered toward the river. Young Tlal half turned, as if to follow Gdeng, but Lithim seized him by the hand and tugged him along. After a short distance, the warriors, as well as the mages, felt their senses clear somewhat. The pull on them was weakening. They increased their speed.

Behind them, and some two hundred paces away, Gdeng was running blindly, almost at top speed. Abruptly, on either side of him, two small figures rose up from where they had been crouching. Gdeng shrieked horribly, as his sense suddenly returned with the impact of a spear ripping into his body. He staggered a few steps and fell, face up. A second spear tore into his throat.

The two hunters stared down at him. Their eyes were yellow and almond-shaped, their faces thin and pointed, their bodies shaggy and incredibly thin. They were like wolves or foxes that had been remolded into humanlike shape. They were no bigger than a human child of two or three.

They were puzzled. Their mage had cast his spell, which would call all creatures within its path to come to him, and the hunters had strung themselves out in a line and crouched down to wait. Much of the morning they had waited, until finally they saw a large pack of wolves, their brothers, trotting along the river. The spell would make the wolves come to them, of course, but the hunters would simply let them go by, for they did not hunt their brothers. But the wolves had not behaved at all as they should. They had stopped, and only one of them had yielded to the spell, while the others had turned and fled. But then, the wolf who was running toward the line of hunters had suddenly changed into one of the large creatures that called themselves humans. Almost automatically, the two hunters on each side of him had killed him as he passed between them, then had waited, half fearing that he would change back into a wolf and they would be cursed for having slain a brother. When he did not change, they suddenly realized what had happened—the wolves were actually humans under a shape-change spell.

The magician leading the hunting band made a high-pitched sound like a trumpet note. At once, a dozen more hunters arose from where they were crouched. In a long, curving line, the small, shaggy figures sped after the fleeing humans.

The men, woman, and boy had a long head start, but they were burdened with their backpacks, and they were not as fleet as the little creatures racing toward them. Glancing back, Lithim saw that the gap between the humans and their pursuers was rapidly narrowing. To make matters worse, his father was in trouble. Mulng was even older than Rlna, and this was beginning to tell; he was starting to fall behind the others. "Father!" said Lithim anxiously, hoping to spur Mulng to greater effort.

Natl, too, realized what was happening. Within another hundred paces, she judged, the Little People would have Mulng in spear range!

She halted and whirled to face them. Swinging her staff in a broad arc, she concentrated her body's energy along a path of power. A long, high line of flame, extending from the riverbank outward to a hillside, exploded up out of the earth just in front of the Little People hunters. The creatures recoiled from this barrier, showing pointed teeth in snarls of frustration.

Natl sprinted to Mulng's side and grasped his arm. "That will stop them for a moment or two," she yelled. "Keep going." He said nothing, but his eyes flicked to her face. He was silently cursing aging legs that would no longer perform as they once had. He wasn't out of breath; he simply couldn't move as fast as the others.

Tremendously grateful for Natl's help and quick thinking, Lithim took another backward glance. The little creatures were trickling around the edge of the fire wall now, but Natl's magic had enabled her companions to gain a good fifty paces on their pursuers. However, the boy knew, with a sinking feeling in the pit of his stomach, that the Little People were eventually going to catch them; the creatures were simply faster than a human, just as a wolf or horse was faster. His father and Natl might block them temporarily with fire walls and illusions—he could help a bit, too—but he felt sure the tiny warriors would just keep on coming.

"We can't outrun them," he yelled. "We're going to have to stop and fight!"

"No!" barked Mulng. He suddenly altered his direction. "The river! Get down into the water!"

He's got an idea, Lithim realized. "Get down into the water!" he echoed, his voice a shriek. If anyone could save them, his father could!

Rlna and his men obeyed, altering their direction, and sped down the gently curving riverbank, through the tangle of water plants that marked the edge of the river, until they were knee-deep in water. In moments, Mulng, Lithim, and Natl had joined them. "Get in line, close together," Mulng gasped. Turning toward the riverbank, he raised his staff with both hands and closed his eyes.

Lithim felt a surge of power emanating from his father. Thick gray mist began to billow up out of the water. It curled around the legs and bodies of the humans and spread forward, rolling quickly through the tangle of rushes and cattail stems, rising as it went. In moments, the mages and warriors were surrounded by a cloud of fog that blotted out all vision. Each person could only barely make out those immediately next to him on each side.

"Put your hand on the shoulder of the one to your right," said Mulng in a low voice, from the head of the line. Lithim, standing next to him, clutched at his sleeve and felt Natl's hand close on his shoulder. "Hang onto each other, and let's go," said Mulng.

The first of the Little People hunters to reach the crest of the riverbank stopped dead. A wall of fog was moving

76

up out of the river toward him, a heavy, creeping blanket of gray that extended along the river in both directions for hundreds of paces. The rest of the hunters joined him. Their quarry was completely hidden and there was no way to tell where, in all that oozing gray cloud, they might be. The hunters began to argue in shrill voices, wondering what to do.

Their magician-leader silenced them with a word. He could have led them down into the fog, where they could all use their keen noses to locate the human things, but he felt that could be dangerous. Some of the human things appeared to be powerful magicians, and it was possible that they had some nasty surprises hidden in this fog. He decided to give up the chase; they had the meat of the one human thing they had killed, and that would be plenty. He ordered the others away from the river and led them loping back to where Gdeng lay staring up into the sky with sightless eyes.

Mulng was moving along slowly, with his staff extended before him, swinging it from side to side as a blind man might, feeling to make sure he was following the edge of the river and was not going to lead his line of followers into an obstacle. Lithim, moving behind him with a hand clutching his leather belt, could hear him counting under his breath; Mulng was counting each pace he took. The wizard felt sure the Little People would not dare enter the fog, but they might move alongside it for a time, hoping for their quarry to emerge from it, so Mulng wanted to keep inside the fog long enough to be sure the Little People got discouraged and gave up. He counted a thousand paces, then another thousand, then a thousand more.

"All right," he said in a low voice. "Let's stop now. I'm going to let this fog clear away. I can't take a reading to see if we'll be safe, so we have to be prepared for anything."

The four warriors held their spears at the ready, facing the direction of the riverbank. Natl clutched her staff and Lithim made ready to cast as strong an illusion as he could. Gradually, colors began to show through the grayness around them, then shapes. The travelers found themselves standing knee-deep in the river with a broad green hillside sloping up away from them. There was no sign of any Little People. The sun was almost straight overhead, indicating that it was midday. From the bulrushes along the riverbank, a bird whistled.

Mulng took a deep breath. "I think we're safe for the moment."

Lithim looked at him, seeing his face in profile—the thin, slightly hooked nose, the web of laughter lines at the corner of his eyes, the broad forehead overhung with a protruding thatch of gray-speckled auburn hair, the ruff of gray beard beneath his lips and the bristle of gray moustache above them. His face appeared drawn and tired to Lithim, and the boy understood, suddenly, what a tremendous burden it must be to be the leader of an expedition such as this. I've been depending on him for everything, thought Lithim, and so have the others. But he has no one to depend on except himself. Everything is on his shoulders.

They began to wade toward the riverbank. "You saved us with that spell," said Natl, admiration in her voice. "If we had tried to fight them, some of us would surely have been killed, even though we might have driven them off. But raising that fog was a brilliant idea!"

Mulng grinned. "Actually, I had been wishing for a *real* fog all morning, so the thought was in my mind. I couldn't have done it if there hadn't been a river nearby, though. It requires a lot of water."

"It *was* a good spell, High Wizard," said Rlna earnestly. "Why don't we stay with it? I mean, why don't we just follow the river's edge all the way to the mountains with a wrapper of fog around us?"

"I really don't think that would be wise, Rlna. A fog seeping up out of a river on a bright, sunny day is unnatural. It could draw attention. The Little People obviously have magicians, and there are magical ways of locating things that are within a fog. I think it better if we just trust our wolf images to keep us from being noticed. I'll be more careful about guarding against Little People summoning spells from now on." He hesitated a moment, looking from Rlna to the other three warriors. "I'm sorry about Gdeng. If I had become aware of that summoning spell a few moments earlier, I could have saved him, I think."

Rlna jerked his head. "Don't feel as if it was your fault, High Wizard. Gdeng's luck just ran away. That happens to warriors."

Mulng sighed. "I suppose so. Well, let's keep going."

The afternoon was uneventful. It occurred to the travelers that the Little People probably did their hunting in the morning and occupied themselves with other things, in or near their dwellings, for the rest of the day. If so, the humans would be relatively safe until sunup tomorrow, unless they chanced to pass close to a Little People dwelling.

When twilight settled over the hill country, Mulng called a halt for the night, and they camped close to the river's edge. The warriors, all of whom had considered throwing off their backpacks that morning in order to run faster, were now glad they hadn't, for it would have meant the loss of most of the expedition's provisions, and they would have had to have a meager supper after going all day without food. They devoured dried meat and bowls of gruel, and in addition, from a stoppered clay bottle in her bag of belongings, Natl put a drop of greenish liquid into everyone's drinking water, which made them feel greatly refreshed.

As they squatted in a circle, eating, young Tlal suddenly lifted his head and stared off into the gathering darkness. "Listen!" he exclaimed. In a moment, all the others also heard what had caught his attention—a faint whisper of a drum, far in the distance. It was being beaten irregularly, in an odd pattern without any rhythm. Abruptly, it stopped.

Moments later, much closer and clearer, another drum began to beat in the same odd way. After a time it stopped, and almost at once another drum, from still a different direction, began to sound.

"What could that mean, I wonder?" murmured Rlna.

"We humans don't know much of Little People ways," Mulng answered in a low voice. "They may have some religious ceremony they hold at this time of night."

Lithim wasn't so sure. The drums made him feel uneasy, for he had the odd thought that they were *talking* to one another. "Father," he said, whispering as they all did when they talked so their voices wouldn't carry, "if we're safe in the darkness, why don't we just keep on going all night? We could lie low through the morning tomorrow, taking turns sleeping and keeping watch. Then we could go on during the afternoon and the rest of the night. We'd probably be in the mountains, out of Little People territory, by sunup of the day after tomorrow."

"I don't think it a good idea to go without sleep tonight, young wizard," said Rlna, answering him before Mulng did. "Morning is the time of greatest danger, when we might have to run or fight. A man who has gone without sleep for a long time cannot move as fast or think as well as one who has had a good night's rest."

"I agree with Rlna, Lith," Mulng whispered. "I think we should sleep when we are safest. We'll stay close to the river tomorrow, so that I can call up a fog again for a time if we need it. You and Natl and I will be alert for Little People summoning spells, as you were today. We'll be all right. It's only two more days in Little People territory. We'll make it to the mountains."

But later, lying on his back and waiting for sleep to come, Lithim was still worried. He could not get over the feeling that the drums of the Little People had been talking to one another—talking about the humans who were moving through their land. Talking about catching us and killing us, thought Lithim. Here we are trying to keep them alive by saving the world, and they're trying to kill us. It isn't fair!

After a time, lulled by the steady croaking of frogs along the riverbank and the buzz, creak, and whir of insects calling for mates, he slept.

81

9

In the morning, with dawn just barely streaking the eastern sky with pale color, they gulped down a quick breakfast of gruel and started out again. The land was noticeably rising now; the river seemed narrower and faster-moving as it coursed down from higher ground. The mountains looming across the horizon like a gigantic jagged wall were sharply distinct, the pine forests on their sides showing as a shaggy texture, fissures in patches of bare rock appearing as faint wrinkles, waterfalls attracting the eye as thin threads of shimmering silver. At this distance, the configurations of rock that had given the Old Woman its crone profile several days ago did not line up the same way, and the profile could no longer be seen.

Only once, during the morning, were the travelers alerted. They were moving along just below the crest of the riverbank, so that they could see into the distance, well off to the side, without being very visible. Suddenly, some hundred paces away, a band of Little People appeared from behind a swell of ground, running parallel to them. But it seemed as if the hunters either did not notice them or else ignored them because of the wolf-image spell, for the figures ran on and vanished from sight again behind another slope.

"The Mother's with us," the warrior named Ulnda exulted in a hoarse whisper.

"Quiet!" Rlna whispered sharply, but then added, "It's High Wizard Mulng's *spell* that's with us!"

Nothing more happened, and when nightfall arrived, they threw themselves down to rest, elated. One more day in the lands of the Little People and they would be through to the mountains. By late tomorrow afternoon, Lithim calculated, they would be in a pine forest at the foot of a mountain slope, where, according to what Mage Hlim had told them in Soonchen, the Little People did not set foot.

This night there was no sound of drums, and that added to Lithim's peace of mind. Father was right, he thought; last night must have been some special festival or observance for the Little People that called for a lot of drumming. They weren't using their drums to talk about us at all, the boy decided.

As the next morning wore on with no difficulties, Lithim felt his elation growing and could tell from the faces of the others that they, too, were jubilant. They flashed grins at one another, and their movements were lively. The sun reached its highest point in the sky and began its afternoon downhill slide. Surely, now the worst was over. Surely, they were safe.

And then Mulng, Lithim, and Natl stopped abruptly

and looked at one another with startled eyes. The warriors halted at once, staring anxiously at the three, aware that something was wrong.

"Mage power," whispered Natl. "Mighty Mother, it's *strong!*"

Any magician, whatever his or her degree of ability, acquired a buildup of power from constant use of magical forces. This power, literally wrapped like a cloak about the mage, could be used to heighten spells and perform activities of greater complexity, which themselves served to further increase the mage's power. Mage power could be felt by other magicians, especially when its possessor directed his or her attention directly at them. Mulng, Natl, and even Lithim, although he was not as adept as the two adults, had become aware that a mage of considerable power had detected their presence and was concentrating on them.

"Who could it be?" Natl stared toward the looming mountains. "The Dragon?"

"Too far," answered Mulng, darting glances about. "This is close. It—oh, Great Mother, no!"

He was staring with stricken eyes toward a long, curving swell of ground some two hundred paces away and slightly behind them. A long line of tiny figures had appeared over its crest, moving at a steady trot straight toward the man, woman, boy, and warriors. It was a Little People's hunting band, more than twenty strong.

"He's with them," said Mulng through clenched teeth. "A mage of the Little People, with power as great or greater than mine! He has pierced my spell, knows what we are, and is bringing his hunters to kill us or capture us. He can counter our magic, and in straight combat they outnumber us almost three to one. We haven't a chance!"

"By the Mother's eyeballs, what foul luck," cursed one of the warriors. "We had nearly made it to the feet of the mountains!"

Abruptly, Mulng shook his shoulders, and from that gesture Lithim knew that his father had made a decision. Mulng spoke rapidly. "If we all die here, everything we've gone through is for nothing and everything we hoped to do is destroyed. It is vital that someone at least make contact with that Dragon mage. Natl, perhaps you can do that, but you cannot possibly stand alone against this High Wizard. *I* can, long enough to gain time for all of you. Turn now, and run for the mountains. I charge you to obey me!"

Lithim stared in shock at his father. "No!" he protested. He knew his father was right, but every part of him wanted to stay and fight to help Mulng, too, get safely away. He knew that if he left his father here now, he would never see him again!

Mulng laid a hand on Lithim's cheek and smiled into the boy's tear-brimming eyes. "Lith, never forget that I love you. I pray that the world can be saved so that you will be able to grow up and become a greater wizard than I ever was. Now go, son. Natl, make him go with you!"

Lithim felt his arm seized and in a moment he was being hurried away at a stumbling run by the woman. "He is doing this for you most of all, Lithim," she told him in a broken voice that betrayed her own emotion. "Don't let it be in vain. Run as fast as you can!"

Sobbing, he nodded and broke into a sprint. He

heard Rlna yell, "May the Mother accept you, High Wizard"—the ritual farewell statement to one who was about to die. Turning his head as he ran, the last sight he saw of his father, through blurred eyes, was of Mulng standing with legs widespread and right arm raised in an invocation as he faced the line of small shapes loping toward him. Then Lithim found himself running down the slope of a gentle ground swell, the crest rising behind him so that he could see nothing more.

Lithim sat in darkness, his shoulder against the slim trunk of a pine tree, staring blankly in the direction of the open, hilly country he and Natl and the warriors had left behind—and where they had left his father. They had seen no other Little People during their afternoon run, and they had not been chased by the band that Mulng had stayed to face, so apparently the wizard had sold himself dearly to enable his son and the others to get well away. Shortly before sunset the boy, woman, and warriors had reached the outlying trees of the pine forest that spread up the lower side of the Old Woman, and to be sure they were perfectly safe and beyond all reach of the Little People, they had begun the ascent of the slope, continuing until all light had faded completely and they could no longer see their way. Now, about half a hundred paces above Lithim on the slope, a spot of orange glowed where the warriors had made a campfire.

At their request, Natl had used a summoning spell to lure a deer into range of their spears in the firelight, and they were roasting portions of the animal over the fire. Lithim had come this short distance back down through the woods to be alone with his thoughts for a time.

His eyes were dry now; he had wept himself out during the afternoon. The thought of his father brought no more tears, only a hard, hurting lump in his throat and a dreadful sense of loss. How could he go on, he wondered, without the man who had been his entire world since he was old enough to be aware of things? He leaned his head against the tree trunk and gave a shuddering sigh. What does it matter, he thought dully, if the world ends in less than a year? For me, it ended today.

Nearby, a twig snapped, and Lithim knew instantly that something was moving through the trees toward him. Only a fairly large, heavy creature could break a twig underfoot, so it might be a bear or mountain lion. Lithim was not particularly afraid, and in his present state of mind was not even sure if he would care if he were killed, but he did not particularly want to be ripped by claws and teeth. Concentrating, he formed a Witch Light over his head, which dimly illuminated an area of a dozen or so paces all around him, and looked to see what the creature was. If it were a bear or lion, he would frighten it off with the illusion of a wall of fire.

But it was Natl, an expression of concern on her face. She came and squatted beside him. "Come and eat, Lithim," she urged. "You need to eat something."

Despite fasting all day and running most of the afternoon at a steady trot, broken only two or three times by short intervals of rest, Lithim had no appetite. "I'm not hungry," he told her.

She sighed. "Listen to me, Lithim. I know how you feel. I know how it hurts! It hurts me, too, because I had grown fond of your father. But he did what he did so that we could try to finish what he had started, and we can't let him down. He expected me to get up this mountainside and talk to that Dragon, and I'm going to do my best, but"—she ran a hand nervously through her cloud of blonde hair—"but I'm not the mage he was, Lithim, and I'm going to need all the help I can get! You can help me. He said you could and I'm sure you can; you have as much power right now as a lot of grown-up magicians I've known. But you'll have to put your grief aside to do it, Lithim—you'll have to ignore the hurt and do what your father expected you to do!"

Lithim realized that everything she said was true. He would, indeed, be letting his father down if he simply continued to grieve and did nothing. "All right, Natl," he said. "I'll go eat something. And I'll help you reach the Dragon and talk to it. I'll be all right now."

She gave him a delighted hug, and together they made their way up to the campfire. The portions of deer had apparently been cooked to the men's satisfaction and they were happily gorging themselves, but they had piled two large pieces of bark, hacked from a log, with cuts of the roasted meat, which they quickly offered to the boy and woman. To his surprise, Lithim found that he had an appetite after all.

Natl could not ring the campsite with a protective spell as Mulng had been able to do, so the warriors decided they had best take turns keeping watch during the night, as there were surely many dangerous animals roaming the mountainside forest. As Lithim lay down to sleep, memories of his father filled his thoughts, and tears came to him again.

He awoke shortly after dawn and gulped back more tears at the sudden remembrance that his father was dead. The warriors glanced at him sympathetically, and young Tlal gave him a couple of gentle pats on the shoulder. Breakfast was cold deer meat, and as they were eating, Rlna glanced appraisingly at Natl. "When will you be starting up the mountainside to meet with the Dragon, Lady Wizard?" he asked. Clearly, the warriors now regarded her as leader of the expedition.

"As soon as we finish eating," Natl told him. "I'll want you men to come with us as far as possible as protection against dangerous animals, but when we begin to encounter the Dragon's spells, Lithim and I will go on alone and you can make camp and wait for our return." She hesitated a moment, then continued. "I don't know how long it will take us, and I don't know if we'll even survive it. But I guess if we do not return by the end of five days you can figure that we're dead and start back for Soonchen."

Rlna nodded, saying nothing. As the men were making ready for departure, Natl came to where Lithim sat packing his shoulder bag and knelt down beside him. "Lith, did your father talk to you about what he thought he might run into when he started up the mountain to try to make contact with the Dragon?"

To Lithim, her face appeared haggard and worried, and he felt sorry for her. He remembered how he had suddenly realized what a hard thing it must have been for his father to have to make all the decisions and plan all the movements of the expedition, and now this task had fallen on Natl's shoulders. Lithim felt that she didn't think she was up to it, but she was determined to do her best.

"He talked about it sometimes while we were journeying to Atlan," the boy told her. "He said he thought the most dangerous of the Dragon's spells might be the ones it uses for summoning food animals to it because if you got caught unawares by one of those, you'd lose your will and purpose and wouldn't be able to try to talk with the Dragon when you got to it, and then it would probably just eat you. He thought the other spells would probably be mostly illusions to frighten off big, dangerous animals like cave bears and packs of dire wolves, so a human mage should be able to see through those pretty easily. But"—Lithim smiled faintly at the memory—"once he laughed and said that no human knows how a Dragon thinks, so he couldn't really be sure what the Dragon's spells would be like until he bumped into them, and then he'd have to figure out what to do."

Natl nodded, chewing her lip thoughtfully. "Well, that's just what we'll have to do, too. What will be, will be." She stood up and adjusted her pack. "Are you ready, Lith? Let's go, and may the Mother—and the spirit of your father—be with us!"

The lower slopes of the Old Woman were not steep, and the early part of the ascent was quite pleasant. The pine forest reminded Lithim of the forest he had grown up in, but that brought back memories of happy times with his father, so the boy stayed wrapped in a contin-

91

uous shroud of grief, not speaking with his companions. They all understood and did not intrude.

By midday the trees were thinning out and there were more and more patches of bare rock scattered through the forest. The climb was growing steeper. The warriors began using their spears, and Lithim and Natl their staffs, to help themselves along. In the early afternoon they paused for a time, to rest and to eat some more of the cold deer meat that each had put into his or her backpack.

Continuing on their way, they shortly struck a deer path—a narrow trail worn among the trees by the hooves of countless generations of antlered animals. This made the going easier, for the deer had picked out the best upward route through the trees, but it also led the humans directly into their first encounter with a Dragon spell. Lithim felt his body tingling and realized he was feeling a tremendously strong urge to hurry straight on up the trail at the greatest possible speed. "Natl!" he exclaimed, forcing himself to come to a halt.

"Yes, I feel it," she said through clenched teeth. "Quickly, everyone, get off this path! Move among the trees, to the left."

"But it's easier this way," said Ulnda, speaking more slowly than usual and plodding onward with a foolish smile on his face. "We can be at the top in no time."

"It's a summoning spell, you fool," she shrieked at him. "Like the one that got Gdeng killed! Keep going and you'll be supper for a Dragon! Get off the trail, all of you."

"Count, sing, shout, stamp your feet," urged Lithim,

recalling what his father had taught him about counter-ing such spells. "It will help you get away from it."

It was like trying to walk through hip-deep water to turn and force themselves away from the trail. But the men did as Lithim had advised them, concentrating on singing bawdy songs and shouting great curses, which helped take their minds off the desire that was tugging at them to continue on up the deer path. The farther they drew away from the trail, the easier it became to move normally, and after a few dozen paces they were free of the overwhelming urge that had seized them.

"By the Mother's teeth," swore Ulnda, "that nearly had me!"

"Father was right," Lithim commented to Natl. "We'll have to be on guard against the Dragon's food-sum-moning spells."

"Yes, and we're bound to run into more of them now, as well as other spells," she said, her face grim. She looked at Rlna. "Here is where we had best leave you, warrior-leader. Lithim and I will probably soon have all we can do to protect ourselves, and we won't be able to help you men as we just did."

Rlna nodded and glanced about. They were in a tiny open place among the close-growing trees, where there would be room to make a fire and lie down to sleep. "We will camp right here, Lady Wizard," he said. "We will give you six full days, starting tomorrow morn-ing, before we give you up for lost. Until then, we will keep a fire going, day and night. The smoke will rise above the trees to guide you back to us by day, and the glow will be a beacon for you by night."

"That is well," said Natl. "I hope we'll be able to

make use of it! Now, before we go, I will give you part of the rest of the payment the High Wizard agreed to—just in case we don't make it back." She showed them the spell for summoning an animal to them: how to make a drawing of the kind of animal wanted, the words to say, the moves to make. This would not only keep them well fed while they were waiting here in the forest; it would also make their fortunes as hunters back in Soonchen if they were able to return there safely.

"All right," said Natl when she was finished. "Let's go look for our Dragon, Lithim."

"May the Mother look after you, wizards," said Rlna, a short prayer for safety that was echoed by the other men. Tlal clapped Lithim on the shoulder in a friendly gesture of farewell.

Plodding among the trees a step behind Natl, Lithim was faintly surprised to find that, although he faced an unknown number of probably very dangerous spells, and, if he got through those, a face-to-face confrontation with a Dragon, he really wasn't much afraid. He knew he might well be killed at any time during the next day and a half or so, but that didn't seem to frighten him. His father was dead, and the world itself might be dead within less than a year, so death had lost much of its terror.

However, while Lithim wasn't afraid of dying, he very much wanted to keep on living now. He wanted to live because dying would mean *failure,* and Lithim realized that failure was the thing he feared most. More than anything, he wanted to help Natl be successful in finishing the task his father had set out to do.

The climb was growing steeper, but the trees had thinned out so that they were many paces apart, and it was not difficult to pick an easy path through them. The boy and woman began to encounter huge masses of bare rock, and once they passed a cave, a shadowed opening into the mountainside that Lithim suspected might well be a refuge of a huge cave bear or mountain lion. There was more to worry about on the mountainside than just the Dragon's spells, he reflected; there were many kinds of dangerous creatures for which a human would be a tasty meal. He and Natl could probably handle most such creatures by befuddling them with an illusion—unless a creature managed to sneak up on them or attacked from ambush, not giving them time to make use of their magic. The boy began to scrutinize the landscape very carefully, watching for places where animals might hide.

He and Natl were definitely *climbing* now, rather than

simply walking upward. They had to lean forward slightly to keep their balance and use the butts of their staffs, jammed against the ground, to help pull themselves along. It was hard, thirsty work, but they allowed themselves only an occasional mouthful of water from the leather water bags they each carried, for they had no idea how long the climb might take and did not want to risk running out of water before they reached their goal.

Perhaps because he was younger and just a bit more limber and active, Lithim found himself in the lead, Natl a few paces behind. Thus, it was he who encountered the next Dragon spell. Working his way cautiously around a boulder, he stopped short at what he saw and waited for the woman to reach him. Just ahead of them was a hissing, crackling wall of fire, three times the height of a human, which apparently stretched across the entire mountainside. They could feel the blast of its heat.

"An illusion," Lithim pointed out, just a trifle contemptuously, for he had really expected something more spectacular from the Dragon. "It's burning on bare rock and not giving off any smoke." Of course, the line of flame would terrify any animal but, as his father had said, a human mage, or, for that matter, any human, thought Lithim, could easily see through the trickery.

Natl sighed. "Well, it won't burn us, of course, but it's going to hurt going through it; you know that, don't you, Lith?"

He nodded. An illusion such as this affected a viewer's senses, so that not only was the fire seen and its crackling heard, but its heat was also felt. "I don't imagine it's very thick, though," he said hopefully.

Natl sighed again. "Let's get it over with."

They scurried as quickly as they could toward the blazing wall and plunged into it. They experienced a few seconds of agonizing pain; then they were through, standing on the other side, the slope stretching out behind them and not a sign of the fire, for the illusion did not exist from this direction.

"That wasn't too bad," said Natl, although she was rubbing her bare arms, in memory of the pain they had felt. "Let's hope everything else we encounter will be just as easy."

They continued on. Some time later, to their delight, they came to a narrow trickle of water, coursing its way down from the giant mass of melting snow on the mountaintop, following a path that eventually joined with other trickles to form the river that flowed through the territory of the Little People. Gratefully, Lithim and Natl drank their fill and filled up their water bags.

The sun was low in the sky now. Natl peered upward at the gray heights rising above them. Clearly, they weren't going to be even halfway to the top of the mountain by sunset. She glanced about. "We should start looking for a sheltered spot to spend the night," she suggested.

They plodded onward. The slope upon which they moved was covered mainly with low-growing plants out of which an occasional bump of bare rock arose. Coming to one such bump, a long, high ridge, they saw that there was a kind of natural dent in it, forming a shallow "cavelet" no more than a few paces deep and just wide enough for two people to shelter in. "There," said Lithim, pointing it out. "We could spend the night there. Nothing could get at us from behind or from the sides very easily and we could make a circle of fires to keep anything from coming at us from the front."

"I don't think we'll find anyplace much better," Natl agreed. "Even though there's still enough daylight for us to keep going for a while, I think we ought to stop here."

They busied themselves for a time, collecting brushwood, which was scarce in the area, and piling it in a semicircle before the niche in the ridge of stone. When they had found all they could, Natl appraised the curving pile of twigs, branches, and bark thoughtfully. "There's not enough here to keep burning all night," she decided. "I wonder if we hadn't better take turns keeping watch, like the warriors do? We could split it up, half a night for each of us. That wouldn't be too bad."

Lithim pondered. It seemed to him that they both ought to get all the sleep they could; he remembered Rlna's warning that a sleepy person could not think and move as quickly as one who was fully rested. "Natl, I believe I could cast that spell my father used for putting a wall of protection around us when we were in the land of the Little People. It would be there to protect us if the fire went out. I know how Father does it—did it. I don't have nearly the power he had, but I think I have enough."

"Go ahead and try," urged Natl.

Lithim closed his eyes and took several minutes to concentrate on gathering all his power together, as his father had taught him to do when he was still a toddler. In his mind he formed two symbols, that for a wall or barrier and that for fire, and fixed his full attention on them. Then he began to slowly march in a semicircle several paces outside the piled firewood, softly chanting the words and making the motions with his staff that he had learned from watching his father every night during the long journey from their home to the coast, which had mainly been through dangerous forest. The words, spoken in the tongue of wizardry, told how his footsteps were forming a line that was a barrier and that anything attempting to cross that barrier would suddenly see and feel it as a wall of flame. The movement of his staff gathered his accumulated power into an invisible curtain that followed the line of his footsteps and hung over it.

Completing the incantation, the boy stepped over the firewood and joined Natl, who had seated herself in the niche, her back against the rock wall. She eyed him with distinct respect. "Your father was right, Lithim. When you grow up, you're going to be a powerful wizard indeed!"

"*If* I grow up," he said, making a grimace. "If none of this works—if we can't get all the mages of all the races to work together as Gwolchmig the Troll hoped, to make a great magical weapon to fight off the Sky Creatures—the world will be destroyed and I'll never *get* to grow up!"

"Well, we're doing what *we* can to help make the weapon," said Natl, patting his hand comfortingly. "And you can be sure that Gling and Ulnr and most of the other mages are doing as much as they can, too. We'll do it, Lith. We must!"

99

For supper they ate the last of their deer meat. When full darkness was beginning to gather, they set the semicircle of brushwood ablaze using commonplace flint and iron as ordinary people did, rather than magic, in order to conserve their power. Sleep came easily, for they were both fatigued from the climb up the mountainside.

They were startled out of sleep sometime during the night by an earsplitting squall of pain and the sound of heavy, pawed feet pattering rapidly away. The fire had indeed burned itself out as Natl had predicted, and something had obviously tried to get at them, but Lithim's spell had driven it off. Confident of their safety, they slipped back into slumber.

In the morning, after a breakfast of acorn gruel, they started their climb again. It was now becoming distinctly difficult and, in places, slightly dangerous. Once they had to inch their way along a narrow ledge, looking down into a fissure many paces deep, where a fall would have surely meant a broken arm or leg, or worse. They rested for a time after this ordeal beside an oddly shaped boulder, then went grimly on. The mountain seemed to tower an interminable distance above them.

"I wonder if the Mother-cursed beast lives at the very top," panted Natl. "It'll surely take us at least another day and a half to get there."

"There's snow at the very top," Lithim pointed out. "I don't think he'd live in the snow." Somewhat apologetically, he added, "He may live *close* to the top, though."

They struggled on. After a time they came to a peculiarly shaped boulder and Lithim stopped short, regarding it. "Natl," he said with puzzlement in his tone, "this looks just like the boulder where we stopped to rest after we passed that gully." Moving around it, he peered past it, down the slope. "And there's the gully! We've come *backward!*"

"How could that be?" the woman exclaimed. "We've been climbing upward all along. We couldn't have—" Her eyes widened with understanding. "It's another Dragon spell. He made us go in a circle somehow, and we never noticed."

"Let's try again," urged Lithim. "Now that we know about it, we ought to be able to break free of it just by making sure we keep looking straight up the mountainside."

Again they started upward, this time keeping their eyes fixed on the rising slope. Everything seemed to be going well; they could distinctly see features that they had become familiar with, which were high up on the mountain, and they were heading straight toward those features. With rising spirits, they struggled upward.

And found themselves once again approaching the oddly shaped boulder.

"Mother rot him," snarled Natl. "I never heard of a spell such as this. How does he do it?"

"I think we're going to have to go back down a bit, Natl," said Lithim. "Down past the gully and start over. I think we'll have to look for a different way up." He glanced about uneasily. "I don't like this. It could be a trap! The Dragon could keep animals wandering around in this spell until he was ready to come and eat them. I think we've got to get away from it."

"I think you're right," she agreed. "I don't like having

to pass over that gully again, but I guess we have no choice. And I hate to think of all the time we're losing!"

With the boy at her heels, she started around the boulder. Suddenly they became aware of a vast shadow passing over them and instinctively glanced up. Gliding in diminishing circles with its great wings outspread, a Dragon was descending upon them like a gigantic bird of prey swooping down upon a pair of startled rabbits.

12

This is how it ends, thought Lithim bitterly—eaten by a Dragon! For there was no doubt in his mind that the Dragon mage, Klo-gra-hwurg-ka-urgu-nga, had arrived to feed upon the "animals" that had become trapped in his maze-spell.

There was certainly nothing they could do to keep from being eaten, it seemed to the boy. They could not possibly fight so gigantic a creature. Lithim had known that Dragons were huge, but he could not have realized, without actually having seen one, just how huge they really were. This Dragon's outstretched wings could have covered a row of more than a hundred men standing shoulder to shoulder; its snakelike body was half again as long as its wingspread; its legs were as thick and massive as tree trunks; its head was as big as the entire body of a giant cave bear. It was covered with pebbly golden-brown scales that, Lithim felt sure, could probably turn aside the hardest spear thrust of the sturdiest warrior alive and break the stone spearpoint in the process.

Can we fight him with magic? wondered Lithim. What sort of illusion might frighten or confuse a Dragon? Then the boy realized the folly of such an idea, for the mage power that cloaked the Dragon was so strong that Lithim could feel it as a force beating against him. This Dragon was not only an invincible beast; it was also a tremendously powerful wizard, against which any magic that Lithim and Natl might muster would be as nothing. There is no hope, Lithim decided bleakly.

Using its wings as brakes, the Dragon settled on the mountain slope no more than a dozen paces or so from where the boy and woman stood, with a swirl of wind and a jarring impact that knocked the two sprawling. Lithim stayed where he had fallen, stoically waiting for the monster to reach out with one of those huge-taloned, three-toed feet and seize him.

But Natl scrambled to her feet. She was determined to try to carry out Mulng's mission of communicating with the Dragon mage. If I can get its attention, she thought; if I can make it understand why we're here, maybe it will listen and not eat us. I've got to try!

In all of history, only one human had ever talked with a Dragon. That had been the legendary High Wizard Mlingen, who had lived centuries ago, during the formation of the Atlan Domain. Everything that humans knew of Dragons, Mlingen had learned during his brief conversation with a very young Dragon calling itself Hwo-kla-urgi-gra, which Mlingen had written down in a series of scrolls known as *The Book of the Dragons*. The only trouble was, Mlingen had not explained how he had managed to communicate with the reptile. But, reasoned Natl, Mlingen was an Atlanian, and he must have spoken to the creature in his own tongue, so Dragons must be able to understand the Atlan language.

"Dragon mage!" she shrieked. "We are mages also. We come to you about the Foreseeing that showed the death of our world. We can help each other prevent this!"

Klo-gra-hwurg-ka-urgu-nga gave no sign that he had even heard her. He sprawled upon the stone slope, silent and unmoving, regarding the two humans out of unreadable golden eyes, as if, perhaps, he was deciding which to seize first.

Natl tried again. She lifted her staff and waved it back and forth. "Dragon mage! Mages are joining together to fight against the creatures coming to destroy us. Will you join with us?"

Motionless, the Dragon continued to stare at them.

Lithim rolled over and got to his knees. He had become aware of odd stirrings in his mind. Images and patterns that did not seem to *belong* to him were slipping in and out of his thoughts. It was a faintly familiar sensation, but he could not quite remember where he had felt it before.

Then it came to him. It was like when he had touched minds with Udgee, the badger who had been the Watcher at his father's home in the northern forest. He felt sure that someone or something was trying to touch minds with him, and it could only be the Dragon! Lithim closed his eyes and put his mind on the path of concentration his father had taught him when he was six years old. Suddenly his consciousness was flooded with patterns that were oddly alien and occasionally somewhat puzzling, but that formed into understandable communication.

"This one knows/is aware/realizes you seek him. None of your kind has ever done such a thing. This one wonders/is curious/would know why you do this."

Well, at least he doesn't seem to intend to eat us, thought Lithim, greatly relieved. He seems friendly! The boy channeled his thoughts back to the giant creature. "We have come to talk with you about the Foreseeing that showed the end of the world."

"The Foreseeing? This one has deeply deliberated/ greatly pondered/long considered that. This one would know/hear/listen to your thoughts/ideas/considerations about it." There was a distinct feeling of excitement to the Dragon's patterns.

Lithim broke contact and turned to his companion. "I've reached him with mind touch, Natl," he told her. "He's friendly! He wants to listen to us. You can talk to him with mind touch. Go ahead."

She looked at him with an expression of dismay on her face. "Mind touch? I can't do that, Lithim. You'll have to do the talking for us!"

The boy stared back at her, mouth agape. He had never dreamed it might happen, but he realized that everything had suddenly fallen upon *his* shoulders, and the whole purpose of this expedition, the whole success or failure of gaining the cooperation of the Dragons—and maybe of saving the world—was now up to *him,* a twelve-year-old apprentice mage!

"All right. I'll do my best," he nervously assured Natl. But I hope I don't mess things up, he thought.

Taking a deep breath, he redirected his mind onto the path of communication with the Dragon. "Great One, as you must know, the creatures that are coming to us out of the sky seem to have powers that are too strong for ordinary magic to overcome. But both the Troll High Wizard, Gwolchmig, and my fa—and the human High Wizard, Mulng, felt that the Foreseeing showed there might be a way of stopping the creatures. That way would be for the mages of all the races—Dragons, humans, Trolls, and the rest—to join together and combine their magic against the Sky Creatures."

Lithim was prepared to continue, presenting the best arguments he could think of to convince the Dragon of the soundness of the idea of joining forces, but the giant reptile's thought patterns interrupted him, pouring into his mind. *"This one agrees with/concurs with/accepts that belief. This one has pondered/thought upon/considered how to communicate with your kind and others, to suggest just such a joining/uniting/mingling of efforts. But there were many problems/difficulties/barriers. This one is delighted/gladdened/rejoicing that you have come to him with a similar suggestion."*

Lithim could scarcely believe what the Dragon's thought patterns were revealing. He had expected to have to desperately argue and plead with the reptile to accept the idea of joining forces with the mages of other races, and here the Dragon had already arrived at that idea on his own! It astonished the boy to find that this gigantic, monstrous, completely alien being seemed to think in exactly the same way as Gwolchmig, Mulng, Natl, and other non-Dragon mages. Maybe being a mage *meant* thinking a certain way, pondered Lithim.

107

At any rate, it seemed clear that a lot of human attitudes about Dragons being cold, passionless, unfathomable creatures were very wrong. Lithim found that he was beginning to think of Klo-gra-hwurg-ka-urgu-nga as a kindred fellow-being!

"Then you will be willing to work with humans, and you will get other Dragon mages to work with us?" he communicated eagerly.

"This one is prepared to do that," came the promise-conveying thought. *"But this one would know/hear of/ be informed about what the mages of your kind are doing, so that he can then report to/inform/explain to the other mages of his kind."*

Lithim briefly considered how to respond to this request. He decided there was no point in going into the problems posed by the priestesses of the Mother and the High Chieftain of the Atlan Domain. The Dragon probably wouldn't understand such complications of human society anyway. The boy decided to simply present the situation as it had stood when he, his father, and Natl had left Atlan Isle.

"When we left our land to come and seek you," he communicated, "human mages were beginning to form groups to plan ways of fighting the Sky Things. The Troll mages are doing the same, I guess. And the Troll High Wizard, Gwolchmig, was going to try to contact the Alfar, to see if they will join in the effort."

"This is well," came the Dragon's thought patterns. *"The plans/ideas/thoughts of each can be considered/ examined/weighed by the others, and that which is best will emerge."* Then there was a pause, a blur of impressions, as if the Dragon were rapidly going over some-

thing in its mind. *"But there must be a way of communication over distance, so that each will know/be aware of/understand what the other does and needs. Do you intend to return now to the realm of your kind, to inform/assure the other mages that we of the Beautiful People will join/unite with/take part in the effort against the Sky Things?"*

"Yes. They will be glad to learn that," replied Lithim, filing away in his mind the knowledge that the Dragons' name for themselves was apparently "the Beautiful People."

"Then you must take a way of communication back with you." Abruptly, the Dragon's thoughts were gone, and Lithim had the feeling they were being directed somewhere else. He let a sigh of satisfaction hiss between his lips and sank to a cross-legged position on the ground. He simply couldn't believe how easy it had all been.

"What in the name of Mother is happening?" demanded Natl, almost writhing with anxious curiosity. For several minutes she had watched Lithim and the Dragon do nothing but stare silently at each other.

"Well, everything's fine," said Lithim, a trifle smugly. "He agrees with the plan of joining forces and he'll get the other Dragon mages to help, too. Right now he's working out some way for us to keep in touch when we're far apart, I think. You see, mind touch only works when you're close together."

She settled down beside him. "Lithim, you're a wonder. That protection spell last night and now this. I don't think even your father realized what tremendous mage talent you have! Everything would have failed if you hadn't been here."

The boy felt his lip tremble. So much had happened during the past day that he had managed for the most part to put aside the memory of his father's death, and now the sudden recollection brought a wave of grief. He fought it back. "Father could have done it," he said. "He taught me how to do mind touch with animals when I was still little. It's easy."

She shook her head. "Very few mages can do that, Lithim. It's something you have to be born with. Your father could have done it, yes, but—he isn't here. You are, thank the Mother!"

"Well, anyway, it's done," he said and sighed. "We were all so worried about doing it, and it turned out to be easy. I found that Dragons are a lot like people. At least, this one is, and I'd make a wager that they all are. Even though he was sitting in front of me, huge and ugly and frightening, I simply felt as if I was talking with another human." He narrowed his eyes, as a recollection entered his mind. "You know, that's what Father said about the Troll wizard, too. I wonder if, as we get to know these other creatures that we've always hated, we'll find out that we've only hated them because they *look* different from us. Maybe we'll all be able to get along better after this trouble is over—if the world's still here."

"I doubt that you could ever get the Daughters of the Mother to stop hating Trolls and Dragons," said Natl, "or High Chieftain Tlon, either."

Lithim started to say something; then Natl saw his eyes widen as he gazed past her, looking upward. Turn-

110

ing, she saw that a large shape was skimming over the mountainside, speeding toward them through the air. It was another Dragon.

But as the creature grew near enough to be clearly seen, Lithim and Natl observed that it was quite different from Klo-gra-hwurg-ka-urgu-nga. Whereas he was bronze-colored, this Dragon was a silvery green. And it was far, far smaller. I wonder if it's a young one, thought Lithim.

It glided down to land on the mountainside a short distance behind the bigger Dragon. Furling its wings, it stared at the two humans. Like the other, it had golden eyes. Even though it was considerably smaller, it was still an enormous creature, probably at least some fifty paces long, guessed Lithim. Its head alone was nearly as long as Lithim was.

"That one is Gra-kwo," the now-familiar thought patterns of the larger Dragon told Lithim. *"He is too young to have other names yet. He is a student/learner/pupil of magic."*

He's an apprentice, like me, thought Lithim, looking at the small dragon with interest. Because they were both young and both apprentice mages, the boy felt an odd kinship with the creature, despite the vast physical differences between them.

"Gra-kwo will be the voice/communication/link between the efforts of your kind and us," Klo-gra-hwurg-ka-urgu-nga communicated. *"He will accompany you into the domain of your kind. When communication becomes necessary, he will reach/contact/touch minds with this one."*

Lithim blinked in surprise. Obviously, Dragons could

use mind touch across long distances, perhaps even across *any* distance. That explained why they lived apart from one another, the boy realized. It's not that they don't like to have contact with each other, as we always believed—they can *always* be in contact, with mind touch! They don't have to be close.

The great Dragon mage bent his head down toward him slightly. *"How are you called, small one? What are your names?"*

"My name is Lithim," answered the boy.

The big creature pulled back and seemed to wait. After a moment, a new set of thought patterns entered Lithim's mind. *"This one gives you greetings, Lith-im,"* they communicated. The boy realized the thoughts had come from the small Dragon. They were distinctly different from those of the old Dragon mage; there was a kind of gleeful exuberance to them—a feeling of *youngness.*

"I greet you, Gra-kwo," replied Lithim. He had the strong feeling that he had just met a new, staunch friend.

13

"**W**hat is happening now, Lithim?" Natl asked plaintively. "Why is this other Dragon here?"

"He's coming with us when we go back into the Atlan Domain," explained the boy. "Dragons can use mind touch even when they're far apart, and he'll be our way of communicating with Klo-gra-hwurg-ka-urgu-nga and the other Dragons, so that human mages and Dragon mages will each know what the others are doing."

"He's coming with us?" Natl stared apprehensively at the big silvery-green reptile. "Lithim, I don't think that will be possible. If we walk into Soonchen, or anywhere else in the Atlan Domain, with a *Dragon,* it will cause a panic! The village warriors would probably try to kill him, and there would be a lot of trouble, and that would certainly make the Soonchen chieftain and the local Daughters of the Mother aware of us. I'm sure that the news of what happened on Atlan Isle will have reached Soonchen by now, and if we show up there with a tame

Dragon, it will be obvious that we've disobeyed the commands of the High Chieftain and the Council of the Priestesses. That would make us instant outlaws and put us under the death penalty! It would be the end of everything we're trying to do. We *can't* take a Dragon back with us anywhere in the Atlan Domain, Lith.''

None of this had occurred to Lithim, and he nodded unhappily, realizing that everything Natl had said was true. Again he felt he did not want to try to explain all these complex human problems to the old Dragon mage, but he certainly couldn't just refuse the offer of Gra-kwo with no explanation, for that might hurt the young Dragon and anger the old one. The boy's mind raced as he tried to figure a way out of the problem. An idea came.

"Gra-kwo," he thought to the small Dragon, "what do you eat?"

"This one hunts and eats many of the furry, four-legged creatures that dwell on the mountainside," he replied. *"Also, some kinds of plants."* His next communication was distinctly tinged with humor. *"This one has never eaten one of your kind, Lith-im, if that is what you fear. But this one would be willing/agree/assent to making a test/trying a sample/taking a bite if you wish to offer one."*

Lithim giggled, but he had his answer. He looked back at the woman. "Natl, I *can't* tell them we refuse to take him back with us. It might spoil everything if we offended them. But I have an idea. When we get near Soonchen, you and the warriors go on into the village, and Gra-kwo—that's the small Dragon—and I will camp in the woods nearby and keep out of sight. There are plenty of animals for him to hunt, and I'll be all right; I've lived in the woods all my life up till now, and I know how to get food and make shelter." He grinned. "And I'll certainly be perfectly safe because what would try to get at me when I'll have a Dragon with me most of the time? You and that Soonchen mage, Hlim, can get started with what you have to do to contact Gling and the other mages who are working to fight the Sky Things, and I'll sneak into the village once in a while to meet with you and find out if you need to talk to the Dragons about anything."

Natl thought over his suggestion, chewing her lip. "It might work, for a time, at least," she conceded.

"It will work," Lithim promised her. He found the thought of living in the woods with a Dragon for a companion to be tremendously appealing and exciting, but at the same time it really seemed to him to be the best possible answer to the problems Natl had pointed out.

The thought patterns of the old Dragon mage broke into his musings. *"This one will depart now, to begin his task. Much must be done/accomplished/completed, for there are no more than ten turnings of the moon before the creatures of the Foreseeing arrive in our sky. But this one now has greater hope than he had before! Farewell, Lith-im. This one will communicate with you again soon, through Gra-kwo."* There was a pause; then the Dragon mage added, *"You can escape the maze spell by simply going back down the mountain."*

Klo-gra-hwurg-ka-urgu-nga spread his enormous wings with a snap and launched himself into the air with a rush of wind that made Lithim and Natl stagger and

115

wave their arms to keep from falling. In moments, the gigantic creature was dwindling in size as it soared upward in great spirals toward the top of the mountain.

Lithim glanced at Natl. "Well, that's it. The Dragons are going to start working on ideas for fighting the Sky Things, and we can go back to Soonchen."

"Your father would be proud of you, Lith," Natl told him, putting an arm around his shoulders and giving him a hug. "It is fitting that it should be his son who accomplished what he set out to do!"

They started down along the narrow ledge that overlooked the shallow ravine. *"This one will await you below,"* communicated Gra-kwo and, spreading his wings, he flew over the ravine and glided to a landing on the slope beyond. A short time later, the boy and woman reached him, and the three began their descent of the mountainside, the Dragon taking short, mincing steps in order to match the slower pace of the two humans.

Burning with curiosity about Dragons, Lithim began to communicate a stream of questions to the reptile. "How old are you, Gra-kwo? Do you live with your mother and father, as human children do? Are you related to Klo-gra-hwurg-ka-urgu-nga? Are you his apprentice?"

"This one is very young. This one has seen only sixty summers," the Dragon replied, causing Lithim's mouth to drop open in surprise. *"This one does not know his father or mother. None of the Beautiful People knows such a thing. When we hatch from our eggs, we are ready for life and need no care/assistance/supervision, as the young of your kind do. This one does not know*

116

if he is related to Klo-gra-hwurg-ka-urgu-nga, but, yes, this one is that Great One's pupil/student/assistant.'' Then the Dragon had some questions of his own. *"How old are you, Lith-im? This one feels that you are young, as he is. Is that one with you the mother or father of you?''*

"I have seen twelve summers," answered Lithim, wondering what the Dragon would make of the great difference in their ages. "The person with me isn't my mother or father. She is a friend. Her name is Natl, and she is a mage."

"Twelve summers?'' Gra-kwo's thoughts indicated amazement. *"If you were one of the Beautiful People, you would be but a baby, Lith-im! It seems odd/strange/puzzling that we are so much alike but so far apart in years. Of course, the Beautiful People live much longer than you small ones do, so perhaps several of your years are equal to one of ours. You must cram much into so short a time.''* He paused a moment. *"Tell mage Natl this one gives her greetings.''*

Lithim conveyed Gra-kwo's hello to Natl. "Ask him if he has any idea what the Dragons plan to do about the Sky Things, Lithim," she pleaded. "Find out what they know about the Sky Things."

"Klo-gra-hwurg-ka-urgu-nga and other ones long pondered/considered/studied what the Foreseeing seemed to show of the Sky Things,'' Gra-kwo communicated in answer to Natl's request. *"Klo and other mages of the Beautiful People came to feel that the power of the Sky Things is not true magic, but something else—like magic, but drawing upon a different source. It is hoped/believed/surmised that if that source*

can be damaged/affected/disrupted by magic, the Sky Things will be unable to work their will. But that source seems to be stronger than the magic of all the combined mages of the Beautiful People. That is why Klo welcomed your proposal to join forces."

"But what is the Sky Things' source of power?" wondered Lithim.

"Magic, as you know, Lith-im, comes from within the mage. It is his or her ability to concentrate the power of the will to make the forces of nature do things they would not otherwise do. But the power of the Sky Things comes from outside them. They have a way of making the forces of nature work for them. They use the power of lightning as a kind of fuel, to produce light and warmth and to make things move. They will use the power that makes the sun burn to burn our world."

Lithim found himself suddenly wondering which way was better—the way of magic, which benefited only the person who could do it, or this strange "outside" way of the Sky Things, which seemed to be available to all of them. He repeated Gra-kwo's information to Natl.

"I can't understand how the Sky Creatures can do such things," she said, "but somehow we'll have to block them from getting the power they use for what they do. I'll send a message to Gling, urging him to work on that." She cast an appreciative glance at the giant silvery-green Dragon, plodding complacently along only a few paces from her. "It is a very good thing that we were able to make contact with the Dragons. They know much more about the ways of the Sky Creatures than we do, and they'll be of great help. I feel much more hopeful!"

Lithim nodded. Hope was higher in his heart, too, now that the Dragons were definitely involved in the fight. There were still nearly ten moons before the Sky Things were due to arrive, and a great deal could be accomplished in ten moons.

But, he reminded himself, Natl and I have a few serious problems to overcome before we can begin helping with the work against the Sky Things. We're going to have to get safely back through the territory of the Little People, and that won't be easy now that—now that Father's gone. And, first of all, we have to find our way back to where the warriors are camped.

"Do you see the smoke Rlna told us to look for?" he asked of Natl, peering down the mountainside.

She shaded her eyes. "It seems as if it ought to be straight in front of us. The sky is clear, so we should be able to see the smoke rising into it above the treetops." But it was quite a while before they finally sighted a thin thread of gray poking up out of the dark green mass of trees spread out below them like a vast, shaggy blanket covering the mountainside. It was much farther off to one side than they would have thought it would be, and they altered direction to head toward it.

A thought brought a grin to Lithim's lips. "When we get closer, one of us had better go on ahead and warn the warriors that we have a Dragon with us. If we just walk in on them with Gra-kwo, they'll run off like scared rabbits and we'll never see them again."

They camped in the open at nightfall, but there was no need for Lithim to ring them with a protective spell. Gra-kwo informed the boy that Dragons needed sleep only in short snatches every few days, and he would simply lie and meditate through the night while the humans slept, keeping watch, although it was most doubtful that anything would come near them with him there.

As they continued down the mountainside the next morning, Lithim became better acquainted with Gra-kwo, plying him with questions about the ways of the Dragon folk and answering the reptile's questions about humans. It occurred to Lithim that he now probably knew more about Dragons than even the legendary Mlingen had!

By noontime Lithim and Natl were nearing the warriors' camp, and Natl trotted on ahead to let the men know about the Dragon, as Lithim had suggested. He and Gra-kwo had to move more slowly anyway, for the big Dragon often had to fold his wings back and squeeze his way through the close-growing trees.

When the two of them reached the little clearing, the warriors were clustered together and staring apprehensively as Gra-kwo pushed his big, hideous, crocodilian head between two trees and regarded the men with interest. "Never thought I'd be this close to a Dragon and stay alive," commented Rlna. "I certainly bow to you two mages, to be able to make a friend of such a creature!" He glanced from Lithim, who was standing beside the Dragon, to Natl, who was sitting cross-legged with her back against a tree trunk, chewing on something. "Well, what is your wish, wizards? Do you want to start on down the mountain now or wait until morning?"

"Now," said Natl, swallowing, and Lithim nodded. "We may as well get as far as we can into the territory of the Little People before nightfall," Natl continued. "We won't have High Wizard Mulng's shape-changing spell to protect us this time, and we'll have to move as quickly as possible. It will be far more dangerous trying to get back than it was coming through, I fear."

"Perhaps not," Rlna said to her and looked at Gra-kwo. "I'm thinking that having a Dragon with us may be a big help in keeping the Little People at a distance."

"It may keep most of them away," Natl agreed, "but I don't think it would stop that powerful mage that"— she glanced hesitantly at Lithim, then went on—"that High Wizard Mulng fought to help us get away. That mage had more power than Lithim, me, and this Dragon combined! I'm hoping that we can get through his part of the Little People's territory when he and his hunters aren't up and about, so that's why I want to travel as far as we can during afternoon and evening. Let's get started as soon as possible."

"We're ready," said Rlna, commencing to kick out the fire. "I felt sure you and the young wizard would get back to us, so our packs are full of enough smoked meat to last several days and our water bags are filled. We can leave right now."

By late afternoon they were at the foot of the mountain, entering the territory of the Little People where they had left it, traveling alongside the swift-flowing stream. They moved at a steady trot until darkness fell, when they made camp. Gra-kwo, whose big golden eyes could see well in the dark, flew back toward the mountain to hunt for his supper, communicating to Lithim that he would return to them before midnight.

The warriors shared smoked bear meat among themselves and the two mages.

As they were eating, they once again heard the sound of drums suddenly begin throughout the land of the Little People—rattling out a faint question far in the distance, throbbing an answer from somewhere close by, rolling out a suggestion from the other side of the river. Lithim looked toward Natl, a pale shape in the darkness.

"They're talking about us," he grimly told her. "They know we're here!"

14

In the gray light of dawn the six humans and the Dragon started out, moving along the edge of the river so that they would be screened from sight by the rising riverbank, the top of which was far above their heads. Lithim explained to Gra-kwo that they hoped to remain unseen by any of the Little People, and the Dragon was surprised to learn that the humans feared the small creatures.

"Are they not of your own kind?" he asked. *"We of the Beautiful People always thought they were. You and they look just alike to us."*

"They're smaller," Lithim told him, "and they're different from us in ways I suppose you wouldn't notice. But, anyway, they hate us and they will kill us if they can. They"—he gulped and fought tears—"they killed my father as we were coming to your mountain."

"Perhaps it would be helpful/useful/of value if this one flew a short distance ahead and observed the land," the

Dragon suggested. *"If this one sees any of these small ones heading toward you, he will return with a warning."*

This seemed like a good idea to Lithim, and when he repeated it to Natl and the warriors, they agreed. So Gra-kwo launched himself into the air and was soon but a speck in the sky, some distance ahead.

It was midmorning when they saw the speck suddenly wheel and turn back toward them, growing in size as the Dragon sped to rejoin them. "This means bad news, I fear," muttered one of the warriors.

Bad news it was and, dropping near them with a ground-jarring thud, Gra-kwo communicated it to Lithim. *"There is a group of eight of the small ones heading straight this way."*

"Only one more of them than of us," commented Rlna when Lithim reported this, "and the Dragon's teeth and claws ought to be worth half a dozen spears. If you wizards can befuddle the creatures in some way, the lads and I and the Dragon could charge them and probably drive them off."

"How do these small ones kill their prey?" Gra-kwo asked of Lithim.

"They have poisoned spears," Lithim told him. Realizing the Dragon might not know what a spear was, he pointed at one held by a warrior. "Sharp-pointed sticks like that, with the points smeared with poison."

"Such devices could not penetrate/puncture/enter this one's skin," declared the Dragon. *"If all of you were to stand behind this one, you would be protected from the hurling or thrusting of the devices. And if the small ones*

should attempt to come at us, this one will simply oblit-
erate/eliminate/destroy them."

"With your teeth and claws?" asked Lithim, thinking
of Rlna's evaluation of Gra-kwo's fighting abilities.

"By the First Egg, no," replied the Dragon, his
thought patterns indicating contempt for anything so
crude. "Like this." Turning his head toward the stream,
he opened his jaws wide and emitted a gout of fire from
his mouth that shot some twenty paces into the water,
sending up an explosion of white steam.

"Mighty Mother, what's he doing?" exclaimed Natl,
who of course knew nothing of what the Dragon had
been telling the boy.

"He wants us to stand behind him so we will be
protected," Lithim explained. "The Little People's
spears can't hurt him, and if they try to charge us, he'll
shoot fire at them, as he just did."

Rlna took a deep breath, like a man who has suddenly regained hope when all hope had seemed lost.
"Truly, having this Dragon with us is going to be of
great help," he asserted and urged his warriors into
position behind Gra-kwo's broad body.

"How did you do that with the fire?" Lithim asked,
taking up a position beside the Dragon's foreleg, close
to his head.

"It is a spell known to all mages of the Beautiful
People," Gra-kwo told him. "This one does not think
your kind could do it, Lith-im. Our bodies are too different."

Crouched behind the fortress of Gra-kwo's big, scaly
form, the humans waited. Suddenly a row of eight tiny
figures seemed to pop into existence at the top of the

riverbank, which rose slanting up from the edge of the stream.

The humans tensed, awaiting a rain of spears. Gra-kwo, his long neck curved toward the little creatures, surveyed them with his golden eyes. Their own almond-shaped yellow eyes returned his gaze with no trace of fear. Several of them jabbered to one another, as if making comments about something that interested them.

Then, abruptly, they were gone.

Rlna gave a startled grunt. "What in the Mother's name does this mean?"

"It may be a trick," suggested the young warrior Tlal. "Maybe they're just hiding on the other side of the ridge, waiting for us to come out from behind the Dragon and start moving again. Then they'll attack. Why don't I sneak up and peer over the edge of the bank and see if that's what they're up to."

"Go ahead," agreed Rlna. "But take care!"

Tlal trotted out from behind Gra-kwo and ran up the slope of the riverbank. Near the top, he dropped onto his belly and crawled the last few paces, cocking his head so that he could peer over the edge of the bank with just one eye and only a tiny portion of his head showing. But after a moment, those below saw him lift his whole head and stretch his neck to stare into the distance. "They're gone," he yelled. "They're running off in another direction. They're nearly out of sight."

"They must have been too afraid of Gra-kwo to make an attack," suggested Lithim, as Tlal came hurrying back down the slope.

Natl was gnawing her lip, a habit of hers when she

was thinking over something that was particularly worrisome. "I don't know. There was something just—not right about the way they acted. It gave me the feeling that they weren't particularly concerned about us, that they were simply leaving us for someone else to deal with."

Lithim looked at her, his expression bleak. "You mean that powerful mage who killed Father?"

"Yes, Lithim, that's who I mean," she said, worry in her voice.

"I hope he does come after us," said the boy between clenched teeth. "I want to fight him! I want to avenge Father!"

Tlal clapped him on the shoulder. "That's the way to be, Lith. By the Mother, you would make a fine warrior!"

Natl put her head down and said nothing. She knew that if the mage of the Little People came against them again, they would have no hope. As she had remarked earlier, that mage was more powerful than she, Lithim, and Gra-kwo combined. He could launch a magical attack that would strain the three of them to their utmost, and while they were concentrating on defending themselves against him, his little warriors could easily dispatch Rlna's men. The Dragon might be able to get away in the end, but the rest of us would be a feast for the Little People tonight, she thought bitterly.

Gra-kwo touched minds with Lithim. *"This one will fly ahead again and watch for other enemies."*

He launched himself skyward, and the humans commenced to move, at a near trot, along the river. The warriors were hopeful, feeling that the presence of the

Dragon had thwarted one attack by the Little People and could thwart others and that their three mages would be a match for the single mage, powerful though he might be. Lithim and Natl were grimly silent, the boy hoping that there would be an attack by the creature who was his most hated enemy, the woman praying that such an attack would not come.

At just about high noon they saw Gra-kwo circling back toward them. Even before he landed he was communicating with Lithim. *"More of those you call Little People are coming. There are many more than before. And there is a feeling of tremendous mage power with them. It is greater even than the power of this one's teacher, the skilled Klo-gra-hwurg-ka-urgu-nga, greatest mage of the Beautiful People! This one fears for us, Lith-im."*

"Perhaps you should go back to your mountain while you still can," Lithim told him. "This is not really your fight."

"Yes, it is," Gra-kwo admonished him. *"If you are all killed here, then the union that has been made between your kind and the Beautiful People will be destroyed. Without it, there can be no hope for our world. This one will fight to keep that hope alive."*

Lithim sent him a thought of gratitude, then turned to Natl. "It is the mage," he told her. "He's coming, with many warriors."

She emitted a sigh that was almost a moan. "Well, we'll just have to do the best we can. Let's get behind the Dragon, as we did before." With a savage gesture, she pushed her hair back. "Mother rot the little demon, why can't he leave us alone? We're not doing him any harm!"

Grimly they waited, staring up toward the edge of the riverbank. After a time, a single figure strode into sight on it and halted, looking eagerly down at them.

A cold wave of shock rolled over Lithim, and he felt as if his heart had stopped. Then, with a howl, he darted out from behind the Dragon and went charging up the slope. "Lith, it may be an illusion!" shrieked Natl, but the boy knew it was not.

"Father! Father!" he howled as he sped upward.

Mulng came rushing down the slope to meet him, and they fell to the ground in a tangled embrace. "I thought you were dead," sobbed the boy, face buried against his father's chest. "I thought you were dead!"

"I know," said the man, stroking his son's head, his own voice choked. "I wish I could have gotten word to you that I was all right, but there was no way. And *I* was worried about *you*, not knowing what was going to become of you on the Dragon's mountain."

Natl, realizing that it was indeed Mulng and not an illusion cast by the Little People mage, had hurried to them and joined Lithim in hugging his father. "But what happened? How did you escape?" she demanded, laughing and crying with joy in the same breath.

Mulng chuckled. "I didn't escape. I was ready to fight the Little People mage and warriors as best I could, when all at once a quavering old voice called out to me in the ancient tongue of magic. It was the mage, urging me to talk before I started throwing Bolts of Power about like a fool. So we talked."

He turned his head and looked upward to where a

crowd of figures now stood on the edge of the river-bank, looking down at the humans. Most were shaggy little male warriors, leaning on slim spears, but one, who bore a mage staff, was an old female with a cloud of snow-white hair and a face creased and seamed with wrinkles. She wore a smocklike garment of animal hide, with fringed hem and sleeves, onto which scores of tiny bird skulls and animal teeth were sewn. She was regarding Natl and Lithim—particularly Lithim—with great interest.

Mulng indicated her. "That is Neeomah, High Sorceress of the Children of the Wolf, which is what the Little People call themselves, I have found. She is a mighty mage indeed! She had viewed the Foreseeing, of course, but she saw some things in it that none of the rest of us did. She saw that a mage would come into the land of the Little People in the guise of a wolf, bearing a message of hope for the world. So when the talking drums of the Little People families began to pass the word of a band of humans moving through the land disguised as wolves, Neeomah knew that the messenger had come, and she ordered the hunters to leave us alone. She and her family were not coming to kill us that afternoon, as we thought; she was coming to talk with me. When she learned of the great plan to unite the mages of all the races against the coming of the Sky Creatures, she pledged the help of the Little People. Messengers have already been sent to other territories, calling on other Little People mages to join in."

"That's just how it was with the Dragon mage," said Lithim, waving his arms in excitement. "He had already decided that the mages of all the races should join

130

together and he was glad we came to him. We've done it, then, Father!" The boy's eyes were shining. "Humans, Trolls, Little People, Dragons—and surely the Alfar will join us all, too! We've made the weapon that can fight the Sky Things!"

"It seems so," agreed Mulng. "It appears as if mages are all much alike in their thinking, and most of them can see that joining their skills with others is the only hope for saving our world. I think you're right, Lith; the weapon has been made!"

"More than one weapon has been made during these past few days, Mulng," said Natl. "Your son has become a mighty weapon, too! It was *he* who made contact with the Dragons and gained them to our cause, and without his magic to protect us, he and I could never have made it up the side of the mountain. He is a mage of power, Mulng, despite his youth."

Mulng looked at his son with eyes bright with pride. "How happy that makes me, Lith! There were times when I feared I was simply cheating you of life by rearing you in the forest, constantly at the edge of danger, and with only me for company. But I always felt that you had the spark of real greatness in you, and now it seems that spark is beginning to burn brightly. You will play a great part in what is to come, Lith; I feel sure of that!"

He stood up. "Come now. I want to introduce you to my Little People friends, and I want you to introduce your Dragon friend to them and to me. We all have much to talk about. There's a great deal to do and not much time before our enemies come at us out of the

Deep. But, by the Mother, we're going to be ready for them!"

Lithim took a deep breath. The dark shadow was still lengthening over the world, but now, at least, it seemed that a light had been kindled that might hold it back!

About the Author

TOM MCGOWEN is the author of more than thirty books for young people. His widely praised fantasy novels include *The Magician's Apprentice, The Magician's Company, The Magicians' Challenge,* and *The Shadow of Fomor.*

Mr. McGowen and his wife live in Norridge, Illinois. They have four children and eleven grandchildren.